ER

COMHAIRLE CHONTAE ROSCOMÁIN
LEABHARLANNA CHONTAE ROSCOMÁIN

1. This book may be retained for three weeks.
2. This book may be renewed if not requested
   by another borrower.
3. Fines on overdue books will be charged by
   overdue notices.

E C

10. MAR 09	16. UG 11	
06. JUN 09,		B
24. JUN 09	19. JAN	
23.	JUL 1	
22. OCT	OCI 1	
09 DEC 0	12 SEP	
02. MAR 11	19. MAR 14,	
14. JUN 11	91. S	

CROCODILE CREEK:
24-HOUR RESCUE

A cutting-edge medical centre.
Fully equipped for saving lives and loves!

Crocodile Creek's state-of-the-art
Medical Centre and Rescue Response Unit
is home to a team of expertly trained medical
professionals. These dedicated men and
women face the challenges of life, love
and medicine every day!

Two weddings!
Crocodile Creek is playing host to two weddings
this year, and love is definitely in the air! But…

A cyclone is brewing!
As a severe weather front moves in,
the rescue team are poised for action—
this time with some new recruits.

Two missing children!
As the cyclone wreaks its devastation, it soon
becomes clear that there are two little ones
missing. Now the team has to pull together like
never before to find them…before it's too late!

Alison Roberts's
THE PLAYBOY DOCTOR'S PROPOSAL
is the first of four continuing stories revisiting
Crocodile Creek. **Look out for books from**
Meredith Webber, Marion Lennox and
Lilian Darcy. Join them every month in
Mills & Boon® Medical™ Romance

With her arms full of the white silk train of Emily's dress and the soft tulle of her veil, Hannah was walking very slowly, her arm touching Ryan's as he held the silk ribbons joining the wreaths on the heads of the bridal couple. They got a little tangled at the last corner and there was a momentary pause.

And Ryan looked at her.

There could be no mistaking the sensation of free-fall. The feeling that all the cells in her body were charged with some kind of static electricity and were desperately seeking a focus for their energy.

Or that the focus was to be found in the depths of the dark eyes that were so close to her own. This was a connection that transcended anything remotely physical. The caress of that eye contact lasted only a heartbeat, but Hannah knew it would haunt her for life.

It was a moment of truth.

A truth she hadn't expected.

One she most certainly didn't want.

She was in love with Ryan Fisher.

THE PLAYBOY DOCTOR'S PROPOSAL

BY
ALISON ROBERTS

MILLS & BOON

Pure reading pleasure

First published in Great Britain 2007
Large Print edition 2008
Harlequin Mills & Boon Limited,
Eton House, 18-24 Paradise Road,
Richmond, Surrey TW9 1SR

© Alison Roberts 2007

ISBN: 978 0 263 19939 0

Set in Times Roman 16½ on 19 pt.
17-0308-51865

Printed and bound in Great Britain
by Antony Rowe Ltd, Chippenham, Wiltshire

Alison Roberts lives in Christchurch, New Zealand. She began her working career as a primary school teacher, but now juggles available working hours between writing and active duty as an ambulance officer. Throwing in a large dose of parenting, housework, gardening and pet-minding keeps life busy, and teenage daughter Becky is responsible for an increasing number of days spent on equestrian pursuits. Finding time for everything can be a challenge, but the rewards make the effort more than worthwhile.

Recent titles by the same author:

THE ITALIAN DOCTOR'S PERFECT FAMILY
  (*Mediterranean Doctors*)
A FATHER BEYOND COMPARE*
ONE NIGHT TO WED*
EMERGENCY BABY*
THE SURGEON'S PERFECT MATCH
THE DOCTOR'S UNEXPECTED PROPOSAL†

Specialist Emergency Rescue Team
†*Crocodile Creek*

Dear Reader

How lucky am I?

To have colleagues who are also my friends, whose skills I have the utmost respect for, and who share a love of the genre and a dedication to making each story the best yet.

To work together and have the challenge of a scope broad enough to link several books and the sheer fun of intertwining the stories of each other's characters is an enriching experience.

So here we are, back in *Crocodile Creek*, and we're throwing a cyclone at our own bit of Northern Australia. Scary stuff!

I'm more likely to experience a bad earthquake or maybe a tsunami where I am in New Zealand, but it's a good idea to be prepared for whatever dramatic turns nature can take, and we can get some bad storms at times.

Here's what you can do if a strong wind warning is issued:

Bring your pets inside and move stock to shelter.
Secure outdoor furniture
Tape across large windows to prevent shattering.
Stay inside during storm.
Partially open a window on the sheltered side
    of the house.
Stay away from doors and windows.
If you have to go outside, watch out for dangling
    and broken power lines.

Is a cyclone enough of a link for our stories? We didn't think so. There's also a little boy called Felixx…

Happy reading

Love

Alison

PROLOGUE

'SHH, now, Felixx!'

'Hush, OK?'

'Silence. We have to have silence for Alanya to get well.'

For days this was all he'd heard, it seemed to Felixx. He crept around on the edge of Alanya's illness, too scared to ask how bad she was, shut away from seeing her except for one or two short visits to the wellness shelter each day, during which he knew he had to be silent or she wouldn't get better fast enough.

Sometimes he asked people, 'How's Mummy?' He liked to call her Mummy because that's who she was. She always wanted him to call her Alanya, because that was her spirit name, but as she couldn't hear him right now, he said 'Mummy' and it helped a little bit.

The silence helped, too. He had to stay as quiet as anything, or she might not get well. He knew that, but it was so hard. The fish on his sneaker helped. Mummy had drawn it with his felt pens. Mostly the bright orange one. She'd done it the day he'd showed her the hole.

'We can't afford a new shoe just yet,' she'd said. 'So let's make it special. The hole can be his eye, see?'

He could poke his finger in the hole. In and out. It was tight at first but now it was easy. His finger went in and out.

In and out.

It helped him to stay quiet. To stop the questions he so badly wanted to ask, like, 'Mummy…Alanya…are you feeling better? Do you need more medicine?'

She didn't seem to be eating very much. They gave her carrot juice to drink, to drain the toxins from her system. How long did toxins take to drain?

Where did they come out?

He was too scared to ask any of these questions, but he listened more than the healing sisters thought. He heard words like 'worried' and 'taking too long' and after this he stayed even quieter, stopped even asking, 'How's Mummy?' in case his talking, even outside the healing shelter, was the thing stopping her from getting well.

Late one night…he couldn't remember, maybe the sixth or seventh night of her illness…he couldn't sleep, and crept over to the healing shelter because there was light coming from its windows. It was cold and his feet were bare and he didn't dare go inside, but he listened underneath the window and heard more words. 'Getting worse' and 'I don't know' and 'ambulance'.

After this, everything got so confusing, when he thought about it he couldn't think the way it had gone. He fell asleep on the couch on the veranda of the healing shelter, and a big car came with red lights. He hid under the blanket in case he got in trouble for being there. He heard men's voices. 'Too late' and 'useless' and 'bloody quack treatments'. Someone found him—Raina, one of the healing sisters—and he pretended to be asleep and she carried him gently in her arms to his bed, and by the time he got there he must have really been asleep because he didn't remember anything else until morning.

Then there were more words—'very peaceful' and 'gone away on the most wonderful journey'—but he was so good, he didn't say anything himself in case it made Mummy... better call her Alanya...in case it made her worse. A lot of boring time went by. He wasn't allowed to see her at all. He had some meals, breakfast and lunch. Were they saying it was Alanya who had gone on the wonderful journey? When was she coming back? He didn't want to ask because that would not have been hushing and staying silent.

Raina sat him down and hugged him and kissed his forehead and told him, 'Your auntie Janey is going to come and get you, sweetheart.'

He didn't know he had an auntie Janey. He wanted to ask who she was and when she was coming but he was so, so good, he stayed quiet and silent and hushed and didn't say a word.

CHAPTER ONE

'YOU'RE *not!*'

'Yes, I am. What's the big deal? It's only a few days off work.'

'You never take days off work. In all the time I've known you, Hannah, and that's, what—three years? You've never missed a shift.'

Senior Nurse Jennifer Bradley collected the paper emerging from the twelve-lead ECG machine and Dr Hannah Jackson cast an experienced eye over the results.

'Bit of right heart failure—there's notching on the P waves but everything else looks pretty good for an eighty-six-year-old. No sign of infarct.'

The elderly patient, who had been sound asleep while the recording was being taken, suddenly opened her eyes.

'Give it back,' she said loudly. 'You're a *naughty* girl!'

The complaint was loud enough to attract the attention of several staff members near the central desk. Heads turned in astonishment and Hannah sighed inwardly. One of them would be her fellow senior registrar, Ryan Fisher, wouldn't it? And, of course, he had a grin from ear to ear on overhearing the accusation.

Jennifer was stifling a smile with difficulty. 'What's the matter, Mrs Matheson?'

'She's stolen my handbag! I've got a lot of money in my purse and she's taken it, the little blonde trollop!'

Hannah heard a snigger from the small audience by the central desk. It would have been a good idea to pull the curtain of this cubicle but in the early hours of a Monday morning, with the emergency department virtually empty, it hadn't seemed a priority.

'Your handbag's quite safe, Mrs Matheson,' she said soothingly. 'It's in the bag with your other belongings.'

'Show me!'

Hannah fished in the large, brown paper bag

ALISON ROBERTS 13

printed with the label PATIENT PROPERTY and withdrew a cavernous black handbag that must have been purchased at least forty years ago.

'Give it to me!'

Hands gnarled with arthritis fumbled with the clasp. The bag was tipped upside down and several items fell onto Doris Matheson's lap. The contents of the opened packet of peppermints rolled off to bounce on the floor and a number of used, screwed-up handkerchiefs were thrown after them.

'There, I told you! There was a *thousand* dollars in here and it's *gone!*' A shaky finger pointed at Hannah. '*She's* taken it! Call the police!'

Ryan wasn't content to observe now. He was standing at the end of the bed. Faded blue eyes peered suspiciously at the tall, broad masculine figure.

'Are *you* the police?'

Ryan flashed the ghost of a wink at both Jennifer and Hannah. 'I've had some experience with handcuffs, if that's any help.'

Hannah shut her eyes briefly. How did Ryan get away with this sort of behaviour? Sometimes, if he was any more laid back, he'd be asleep. What a shame Doris hadn't stayed asleep. She was sniffing imperiously now.

'Arrest that woman,' she commanded.

'Dr Jackson?' Ryan eyed Hannah with great interest. She couldn't help the way the corners of her mouth twitched. This *was* pretty funny. It was just a shame it was going to give Ryan ammunition he wouldn't hesitate to use.

'She's stolen my money.'

Ryan stepped closer. He leaned down and smiled at Doris. One of those killer smiles he usually reserved for the women he was flirting with. Which was just about every female member of staff.

Except Hannah.

His voice was a deep, sexy rumble. *'Really?'*

Doris Matheson stared back. Her mouth opened and then closed. Hannah could swear she fluttered her eyelashes and stifled another sigh at the typical feminine reaction to being the centre of this man's attention. The coy smile Ryan received was only surprising because of the age of their patient.

'What's your name, young man?'

'Ryan Fisher, ma'am.'

'And you're a policeman?'

'Not really.' Ryan's tone was that of a conspirator revealing a secret. 'I'm a doctor.'

The charm he was exuding was palpable. Totally fake but, for once, Hannah could appreciate the talent. It wasn't being directed at her, was it? She didn't need to arm herself with the memories of the misery men like Ryan could cause the women who trusted them. It was certainly defusing a potentially aggravating situation here.

'Ooh,' Doris said. 'Are you going to look after me?'

'You're about to go to X-Ray, Mrs Matheson,' Hannah said.

'What for?'

'We think you've broken your hip.'

'How did I do that?'

'You fell over.'

'Did I?' The question, like the others, was directed at Ryan despite it being Hannah who was supplying the answers.

'Yes.' Hannah looped her stethoscope back around her neck. 'And we can't find any medical reason why you might have fallen.' The cause had been obvious as soon as Hannah had been within sniffing distance of her patient. She hadn't needed the ambulance officer's report of an astonishing number of empty whisky bottles lined up on window-sills.

Ryan was smiling again but with mock severity this time. 'Have you had something to drink tonight, Mrs Matheson?'

She actually giggled. 'Call me Doris, dear. And, yes, I do like a wee dram. Helps me sleep, you know.'

'I'm sure it does, Doris.' Ryan's tone was understanding. He raised an eyebrow. 'But it can make it difficult to remember some things, too, can't it?'

'Ooh, yes.' Doris was looking coy again. 'Do you know, I almost forgot where the bathroom was one night?'

'Did you forget how much money you might have had in your purse, too?'

'I *never* keep money in my purse, dear! It might get stolen.'

'It might, indeed.' Hannah got a 'there you go, all sorted' kind of glance from Ryan. She tried hard to look suitably grateful.

'I keep it in the fridge,' Doris continued happily. 'In the margarine tub.'

'Good thinking.' Ryan stepped back as an orderly entered the cubicle. 'Maybe I'll see you when you get back from X-Ray, Doris.'

'Oh, I hope so, dear.'

Hannah held up her hand as her patient's bed was pushed away. 'Don't say it,' she warned.

'Say what?' Ryan asked innocently.

'Anything about naughty girls,' Jennifer supplied helpfully. 'Or arresting them. And especially nothing about handcuffs.'

'Not even fluffy ones?'

Jennifer gave him a shove. 'Go away. Try and find something useful to do.'

They were both laughing as Ryan walked away. Relaxed. Enjoying the diversion of an amusing incident. But Jennifer could afford to enjoy Ryan's company, couldn't she? Happily married with two adorable small children at home, she was in no danger of being led astray.

Neither was Hannah, of course. She knew too much about men like Ryan Fisher. Great-looking, *fun* men like the ones who'd made her mother's life a misery after her dad died, not to mention the guy who'd broken her sister's heart not so long ago.

Hannah only ever let herself get involved with nice, trustworthy, serious men like her father had been. She'd believed herself to be totally immune to men of Ryan's ilk.

Until three months ago.

Until she'd met Ryan Fisher.

Jennifer was still smiling as she tidied the ECG leads away. 'I still can't believe you're taking time off,' she told Hannah. 'I've never even known you to be sick. You're the one who always fills in for other people like Ryan when *they* take days off work.'

Hannah glanced towards the central desk. Ryan—the king of holidays and all other good things life had to offer—was now leaning casually on the counter, talking to a tired-looking receptionist. Probably telling her one of his inexhaustible supply of dumb blonde jokes. Sure enough, a smile was starting to edge the lines of weariness from Maureen's face.

'I'm going to check the trauma room while it's quiet,' Hannah told Jennifer.

'I'll help you.' Hannah's news of taking time off had clearly intrigued her friend, who didn't consider their conversation finished. 'And there

I was thinking that, if *I* didn't drag you out occasionally, you'd spend all your time off studying or something.'

Hannah picked up the laryngoscope on top of the airway trolley and pulled the blade open to check that the battery for the light was still functional. 'Are you saying I have no life?'

'I'm saying your career takes the prize as your raison d'etre.'

'I always wanted to be a doctor.' Hannah snapped the blade back in line with its handle, switching off the light. 'Now that I *am* one, I intend to be a very good one.'

'You *are* a very good one. The best.'

'We'll see.' The glance between the two women acknowledged the growing speculation within the department over who was going to win the new consultant position. She had been the only serious contender until Ryan had thrown his hat into the ring today. Was that why she was so aware of his presence in the department tonight? Why everything about him seemed to be rubbing her up the wrong way even more than usual?

'Anyway…' The wind had been taken out of Jenny's sails, but not by much. She opened a box of syringes to restock the IV trolley. 'You don't need to prove how good you are by living and breathing emergency medicine.'

'So you're saying I'm an emergency department geek?' Hannah tilted the ceiling-mounted, operating-theatre light so it was in a neutral position. It would be fair enough if she was. Hannah loved this space. Fabulous lighting, X-ray and ultrasound facilities, every piece of equipment they could possibly need to cover the basics of resuscitation and stabilisation of a critically ill patient. Airway, breathing, circulation. To be faced with a life-threatening emergency and succeed in saving that life was all the excitement Hannah needed in her life.

Jenny caught her expression and clicked her tongue with mock exasperation. 'I'm just saying you could do with more in your life than work.'

'And that's precisely why I'm taking a few days off.'

'Touché.' Jenny grinned, magnanimous in defeat. 'OK.' She shoved the syringes into their allocated slot and then used her forefinger to stir the supply of luer plugs and IV connectors, pretending to count. 'So where the hell is Crocodile Creek, anyway?'

'Australia. Far north Queensland.'

'Oh! Has this got something to do with your sister?'

'Yes. I've been invited to a wedding.'

'Susie's getting *married?*'

'No, though I'm sure she'd be over the moon if it *was* her wedding. She's being a bridesmaid to her best friend, Emily.'

'Do you know Emily?'

'No.'

'So why have you been invited to her wedding?'

'Well…' Hannah leaned against the bed for a moment. It wasn't often they got a quiet spell, even at 2 a.m. on a Monday morning and the break hadn't gone on long enough to get boring yet. 'Susie didn't have a partner to invite and we haven't seen each other since she jumped the ditch and came to New Zealand for Christmas. I'm starting to feel guilty about how long it's been.'

'It's only March and it's a hell of a long way to go to ease a guilty conscience. Auckland to Cairns is about a six-hour flight, isn't it?'

'It sure is.' Hannah groaned. 'And then there's the little plane from Cairns to Crocodile Creek, which will take another couple of hours, I guess.'

'It must be a long way north.'

'About as far as you can get. The hospital there is the rescue base for the whole of far north Queensland. That's why I need the Friday on top of the weekend. I have to get right into the heartland of sugar and cane toads.'

'Eew!'

'Actually, it's right on the coast. It sounds gorgeous.'

'You've never been there before?'

'No, and Susie's been living there for as long as I've been working here. It's high time I checked out what my little sister is up to.'

'I thought you were twins.'

By tacit consent, the doctor and nurse were leaving the trauma room, satisfied it was ready for a new emergency. Hopefully, they'd be back in there soon with some real work to do.

'She's four minutes younger than me.'

'And she's a physiotherapist, right?'

'Yeah. She started medical school with me but she hated it. Too much pressure.'

'You must be quite different.'

'Personality-wise, definitely. To look at, no. We're identical.'

'Wow! Do you have, like, that twin thing?'

'Which "twin thing" is that?' They were near the central desk now. Ryan had disappeared, presumably into the only cubicle with a drawn curtain. The nurse on triage duty, Wayne, was sitting, drumming his fingers on the counter.

'You know, when one twin sprains her ankle, say, here in Auckland and the other twin falls over in a supermarket in central London.'

Hannah laughed, dismissing the suggestion with a shake of her sleek head. But was it so ridiculous? Was it just that she was missing a sister who had always also been her best friend or did those niggling doubts about how happy Susie was have a basis in some form of telepathic communication? Was the urge to travel thousands of miles at a very inconvenient time to attend the wedding of two people she only knew through Susie's emails just an excuse?

'Apparently this wedding is going to be great fun.' Hannah tried to find a more rational explanation for the urge she hadn't been able to resist.

'The groom, Mike, is Greek and his parents own a boutique hotel right in the cove. Susie reckons it'll be the biggest party the Creek has ever seen.'

Jennifer's peal of laughter made several heads turn.

'What's so funny?' Hannah's eye was caught by the light on the radio receiver that linked the department with the ambulance service. It was blinking.

Jennifer could hardly get the words out clearly. 'You're going to *My Big Fat Creek Wedding*!'

Grinning, Hannah still managed to beat Wayne to the microphone. 'Emergency Department.'

'Auckland four eight here. How do you receive?'

'Loud and clear,' Hannah responded, her grin fading rapidly. 'Go ahead.'

'We're coming to you from the scene of a high-speed multiple MVA. The chopper's just landing to collect a second seriously injured patient who's currently trapped, but we're coming to you with a status-one seven-year-old boy.'

The grin had long gone. Status one was as serious as it could get. Under CPR, not breathing or uncontrollable haemorrhage were all pos-

sibilities for the priority designation. This ambulance would be coming towards the hospital
under lights and sirens.

'Injuries?'

'Head and facial trauma. Partially unrestrained
front-seat passenger—the safety belt wasn't
latched securely.'

This wasn't the time to feel angry at someone
failing to strap a child into a car seat properly.
Or to wonder why they were travelling at 2 a.m.
in the first place.

'Vital signs?'

'GCS of 3.'

The child was profoundly unconscious. Quite
possibly due to bleeding around his brain.

'Airway?'

'Unsecured.' The paramedic raised his voice as
the siren came on in the background. The vehicle
must be in heavier traffic now. At night, just
having the beacons flashing could be enough
warning of the urgency of their mission. 'There's
severe facial trauma and swelling. We've got an
OP airway in but that's all.'

The boy needed intubation. Securing an
airway and optimising oxygen levels were a

priority in a head injury. Especially in a child because they had a greater chance of neurological recovery than an adult after a head injury and therefore warranted aggressive treatment in the early stages. If the paramedics had been unable to intubate due to the level of trauma, it could mean that this was going to be a challenging case.

Hannah could feel her adrenaline levels rising and the tension was spreading. Nearby staff were all listening avidly and the curtain on cubicle 4 flicked back to reveal that Ryan was also aware of what was happening. Hannah's heightened awareness registered the interest and at some subconscious level something like satisfaction was added to the emotional mix. She was taking this call.

This would be her case, not Ryan's. Just the kind of case she needed to showcase the skills that would be a major consideration in choosing the new consultant for the department.

'What's the oxygen saturation level?' she queried briskly.

'Ninety-four percent.'

Too low. 'Blood pressure?'

'One-thirty over sixty-five. Up from one-twenty five minutes ago.'

Too high for a seven-year-old. And rising. It could well be a sign of increasing intracranial pressure.

'Heart rate?'

'One hundred. Down from about one-thirty.'

Too slow for Hannah's peace of mind. And dropping. It could also be a worrying sign. 'What's your ETA?'

'Approximately five minutes.'

'We'll be ready for you.' Casting a glance over her shoulder, Hannah could see Ryan moving towards the resuscitation area she and Jennifer had just checked. Not that she was about to decline any assistance for dealing with the incoming case but she didn't want Ryan taking over. It wasn't as though there was only one victim arriving, was it? She pushed the button on the microphone again.

'Do you know the ETA for the chopper?'

'Negative. Fire service is on scene, though.'

It shouldn't take them long to cut the second victim clear of the wreckage, then. 'And that's also a status-one patient?'

'Affirmative. Chest trauma. It's the mother of our patient.'

Ryan would be able to lead the team on that case. In resus 2. Or they could share the main trauma room if necessary. Hannah's plan of action was forming rapidly as she replaced the microphone.

'Put out a call for an anaesthetist, please, Wayne,' she directed. 'And let's get a neurosurgical consult down here. Sounds like we might need someone from Plastics, too. Jenny, you're on the trauma team tonight, aren't you?'

'Yes.'

'And you, Wayne?'

'Yes. Resus 1?'

Hannah nodded, already moving towards the area. She pulled one of the protective plastic aprons from the large box on the wall. Ryan was already tying his behind his back.

'Could be a tricky airway management,' he said.

'Mmm. I've called for some anaesthetic back-up but I'll see how I go.' The direct look Hannah gave Ryan could leave him in no doubt that she intended to lead this resuscitation effort. The subtle twitch of an eyebrow let her know the message had been received and understood. It also hinted at amusement rather than intimidation.

'I'll stay until the mother gets here,' he said calmly. 'In case you need a hand.'

'Thanks.' The acknowledgement was perfectly sincere. There was a child's life at stake here and Hannah would never let any personal considerations affect her performance. She would stand back in a flash if she thought Ryan's skills would improve the management. Never mind that he would get the credit for managing a difficult case.

It was just annoying that people that mattered were keeping a count of those credits at present. And disappointing that a competitive edge of any kind had crept into Hannah's working environment when one of the things she loved best about her work was the way a team of people could work together and the only kudos that really mattered was a successful outcome to that work.

The decision on the consultant's position was only a week or two away. A position that represented everything Hannah was striving towards in a career she was passionate about. Why had Ryan decided to compete at the last minute like this? It wasn't as if he really *needed* the position. He didn't have a massive student loan, the repayments of which would benefit enormously from an increase in salary. He didn't need to prove himself in a field that was still dominated by males in senior positions. He was an Australian. Auckland wasn't even his home town.

She couldn't help flicking a glance towards the tall man who had now donned protective eyewear and a pair of gloves and was lounging at the head end of the bed. Why hadn't Ryan Fisher just stayed on his side of the ditch? In that Sydney emergency department where he'd honed his not inconsiderable skills? Life would be so much easier if he had. And it wasn't just due to that professional competition.

Jenny pushed the IV trolley into an easily accessible position and then stood on tiptoe to check that the tubes attached to the overhead suction and oxygen supplies were firmly in place. It was still a stretch for her short stature and Ryan was quick to step forward.

Without a word, he saved Jenny the awkward

task and then gave her one of those killer smiles in response to her thanks. The senior nurse turned back to the IV trolley but Hannah noticed the extra glance that went in Ryan's direction.

Not that he had noticed. The registrar was lounging again, his keen glance taking in the mill of the gathering trauma team and registering the growing tension.

The few minutes before the arrival of a serious case was a strange time. A calm before a storm of unknown proportions. Equipment was primed and ready. Staff were wearing protective gear and waiting. Wayne stood behind a kind of lectern that had the paperwork necessary to document every moment of the resuscitation effort and he was fiddling with a pen.

Hannah had pulled on gloves and was unrolling the airway pack on the top of a stainless-steel trolley. Others were simply standing. Waiting. There was nothing to do until their patient came rolling through those double doors. Nobody liked to speculate in too much detail on what was about to arrive because that could give them tunnel vision. A conversation that required distraction of mental focus was just as unwanted. What usually happened was a bit of gossip or a joke. Light-hearted banter that could relieve tension before it achieved destructive proportions. Something that could be abandoned as easily as begun.

And Ryan could always be counted on to provide a joke that would make everybody laugh.

Everybody except Hannah. She made a point of never laughing at Ryan's jokes because the vast majority of them were at the expense of women with blonde hair. Like hers.

Sure enough, he was telling one now.

'So this blonde—Cindy—is in desperate financial straights and she prays for help. "Please, God, let me win the lottery or I'll have to sell my car." But she doesn't win so she prays again, "Please, God, let me win the lottery. I'm going to have to sell my car *and* my house."'

Everybody was listening. Or half listening. Waiting for the distant wail of the siren that would advertise that the calm was over. Hannah kept her gaze on the trolley, checking that there was a range of paediatric-sized tubes and that the laryngoscope was still working.

She didn't have to look at Ryan to know exactly what the image would be. He would be standing completely at ease with just a hint of a smile and a twinkle in those dark eyes that advertised an upcoming punchline. It might be a terrible joke but everybody would be listening and would be prepared to laugh because Ryan commanded that sort of attention. And popularity. Without even trying.

Hannah lips pressed themselves into a thinner line as she made sure that the more serious gear that might be needed for a surgical airway was at hand. No, it wasn't just the professional competition that irked her. It was the fact that she had been as attracted to Ryan as every other woman who'd set eyes on him from the moment he'd arrived in this department three months ago.

It had been so unexpected. He was the epitome of the type of man she had always steered very well clear of. Despised, even, thanks to the collateral damage she had seen them produce in the lives of women she cared about. One of life's golden people. She had probably been the first woman ever to freeze out an advance from him.

Was that why he was persevering for so long? Did she represent some kind of challenge?

'She *still* didn't win,' Ryan was continuing. 'She's down on her knees, pleading and this time God speaks to her.' His voice dropped to a deep rumble that Hannah could actually feel in her bones. 'And he says, "Work with me here, Cindy. *Buy a ticket!*"'

Sure enough, there was a wave of laughter. A wave that faded with dramatic swiftness, drowned out by the faint wail of a siren. Then the sound of the approaching siren died as it sped onto the hospital grounds with just its beacons flashing. Seconds later, the stretcher appeared. A third crew member was moving rapidly beside the stretcher, a bag-mask unit over the face of the child, trying to keep oxygen levels up on the short journey between the ambulance and the trauma bay.

The team went into action as a unit. The transfer of the small body was smooth—made easier by the fact he was strapped to a backboard with a collar to protect his neck. And although this team was well used to seeing victims of major trauma, it was a shock to get their first close-up view of this little boy.

Waiting at the head of the bed to manage the airway, Hannah sucked in a quick breath that was almost a gasp. No wonder he hadn't been intubated and it would have been far too dangerous to attempt a nasopharyngeal airway. His nose and mouth were almost lost beneath swollen and lacerated tissue. There were obvious facial fractures and the eyelids were so swollen it was impossible to open them enough to assess the pupils with a torch.

'Do we know his name?'

'Brendon,' one of the paramedics supplied. 'His mother was initially conscious enough to be calling for him.'

He was wearing pyjamas, Hannah noticed as she leaned forward. Bright red racing cars on a blue background. 'Brendon, can you hear me?' She reached over his shoulder. Why had he been in a car in pyjamas instead of safely asleep in his bed? 'Squeeze my hand if you can hear me, sweetheart.'

A response hadn't really been expected and Hannah moved swiftly to take the tip of the suction unit Jennifer was holding. The child was moving air but there was a nasty bubbling sound and the probe on his finger revealed an oxygen saturation level that was far too low to be acceptable.

'Rapid sequence intubation?'

'If it's possible.' Hannah's gaze flicked up, relieved to find one of the senior anaesthetic registrars now standing right beside her.

Ryan was on the other side of the bed and farther down, moving in to assess IV access and flow and to look for other potential injuries as the pyjamas were cut clear of the small body.

ECG electrodes were being attached. Jennifer was using a bag mask to assist the delivery of oxygen. Hannah suctioned as much blood as she could from Brendon's mouth and nose.

'I can't see anything that clearly looks like CSF,' she said. Not that that discounted the possibility of skull fractures or spinal damage.

'Saturation's down to ninety per cent. Let's go for the intubation,' the anaesthetist advised. He took the bag mask from Jennifer and began to squeeze it rapidly, increasing the amount of oxygen reserves to cover the down time for trying to get a tube into Brendon's throat. He was clearly prepared to provide back-up rather than taking over the procedure.

Hannah drew in a slow breath to dispel any nerves. She heard herself issue instructions for the drugs needed, like suxamethonium to relax muscles and atropine to prevent the heart slowing dangerously. The formula for determining the size of the endotracheal tube was there instantly—the diameter equalled the age of the child divided by four, plus four.

'I'll need a 6 millimetre, uncuffed tube,' she informed Jennifer. 'And I want you to hold his head while we ease this collar off.'

It was a challenge, easing the blade of the laryngoscope past the swollen lips, broken teeth and a badly lacerated tongue, and Hannah had to use the suction unit more than once. It was an unexpectedly easy victory to visualise the vocal cords and slip the tube into place.

'I'm in.' The tone was one of satisfaction rather than triumph, however. There was still a long way to go but at least they were on the way to stabilising a critically ill patient.

'Well done.'

With her stethoscope now on Brendon's chest

to check for correct tube placement and equal air entry, the quiet words of praise were muted and, for a moment, Hannah thought they might have come from Ryan.

But he was no longer standing beside Brendon. Hannah had been concentrating so hard on her task she had managed to block the sounds of the second patient's arrival and the stretcher was now being swiftly manoeuvred to the other side of the trauma room.

'Blunt chest trauma with tachycardia and hypotension. No sign of a tension pneumothorax.' she heard Ryan stating. 'We could be dealing with an acute pericardial tamponade.'

Would Ryan attempt a procedure to drain off the fluid inhibiting the function of the young mother's heart? It would be a very impressive coup as far as patient treatment if it was successful. Hannah couldn't help casting frequent glances towards his side of the room as she worked with the anaesthetist to get Brendon's ventilator setting right, supervised the amount of IV fluid that was being administered, started an infusion of mannitol, which could help reduce intracranial pressure, and arranged transfer for an urgent CT scan of the boy's head and neck.

Sure enough, Ryan was preparing to intubate his patient, cardiac monitoring was established and kits requested for both pericardiocentesis and chest drainage. Ryan looked determined and confident but less than happy about the challenge he was about to face. And no wonder. From what Hannah could see, the woman's condition was deteriorating rapidly.

Ominous extra beats were disrupting the line of the ECG trace on the screen of the monitor.

There was time for one more, rapid secondary survey on Brendon before he was taken to the CT suite.

'Some of these bruises look old,' she commented.

'Maybe he plays rugby,' Jennifer suggested.

'You reckon his mother does as well?' Wayne had been helping Ryan's team in the initial preparation of his patient. 'She's covered in bruises as well.'

Hannah eyed the clothing remnants Wayne was putting into a patient property bag. 'Dressing-gown?' she queried.

He nodded. 'I don't think their trip was planned.'

A police officer was standing well to one side of the now crowded area. 'Have any relatives been contacted?' Hannah asked him.

'We didn't need to. The car she was driving had just been reported stolen.' The police officer's face was grim. 'By her husband.'

Hannah absorbed the information like a kind of physical blow. Was her patient an innocent young victim caught up in a situation involving domestic violence? Had his mother's desperate bid to protect him ended in a disaster he might never recover from? Would he even still have a mother?

It seemed unlikely. Ryan was sounding un-characteristically tense as Brendon's stretcher was taken through the double doors on the way to CT.

'We've got VF. She's arrested. Charging to 200 joules. Stand clear!' He looked up as he re-charged the paddles. 'Hannah, are you free?'

Hannah's hesitation was only momentary. She had been planning to follow protocol and ac-company Brendon but he already had an expert medical escort in the anaesthetic registrar. She knew what Ryan would do if the roles were reversed and *she* asked for assistance. Hannah turned back.

'I'm free,' she said quietly. 'What do you need?'

CHAPTER TWO

'WE'VE got sinus rhythm.'

Ryan dropped the defibrillator paddles with relief. The same kind of relief he'd noted when Hannah had turned back to help before he'd delivered that last shock. Not that he'd doubted he could count on her in a professional capacity. He could see her pulling on gloves and positioning herself beside the tray containing the pericardiocentesis and chest drain kits as he reached to check his patient's pulse.

'Carotid is barely palpable,' he reported grimly.

'Systolic pressure is fifty-nine,' Wayne confirmed.

'Let's shut down the IV. Just run it enough to keep the vein open,' Ryan ordered. 'There's been no response to a fluid challenge and if we're dealing with thoracic haemorrhage it'll only be making things worse.'

'Ventricular ectopics starting again.' Hannah had an eye on the monitor screen. 'And the systolic pressure is dropping. Down to fifty-five.'

The patient was threatening to arrest again. Ryan reached for a scalpel and Hannah had the forceps ready to hand him a moment later. Then the cannula for the chest drain. In less than a minute, blood was draining freely into the bottle. Too freely. All too soon, the bottle was almost full.

'Have we got someone from Cardiothoracic on the way?'

'No.' Jennifer shook her head at Ryan's terse query. 'Sorry. They're unavailable for fifteen to twenty minutes. They're tied up in Theatre with a post-bypass complication.'

'Have we got a thoracotomy kit?' He could almost hear a collective intake of breath. 'She's exsanguinating from a chest injury and about to go into cardiac arrest again. A thoracotomy might be a long shot but it's the only hope we've got.' Ryan knew the statistics were not on his side but at least they would be doing something other than watching this woman bleed to death.

Hannah nodded once, as though she had gone through the same thought processes and was in agreement with him. 'Want me to scrub as well?'

'Yes. Thanks.'

Wayne was sent to find the rarely used sterile kit. Jennifer took over the task of manually ventilating their patient. Ryan scrubbed fast. Ideally he should have the chest opened in less than two minutes. Faster, if there was another cardiac arrest.

'Have you done this before?' Hannah squeezed soap into her hands beside him.

'Yes. You?'

'Never even seen it.'

'Know the indications?'

'Penetrating thoracic injury with traumatic arrest or unresponsive hypotension or blunt injury with unresponsive hypotension or exsanguination from the chest tube. Overall survival is between four and thirty-three per cent but higher for penetrating injury.'

'We've got VF again,' Jennifer warned.

'No...it's asystole.'

Speed was now critical. A flat-line ECG meant that the heart couldn't be shocked into producing a rhythm again. Chest compressions on someone with blunt trauma were also contraindicated because it could worsen the injury. Opening the chest was the only option with any hope at all now.

It was good that Hannah had never seen the technique. Explaining things as he started this incredibly invasive procedure somehow eased the tension of a desperate measure to save a life.

'We'll make bilateral thoracotomies in the fifth intercostal space, mid-axillary line—same as for a chest drain.' Ryan worked swiftly with a scalpel and then a heavy pair of scissors. 'I'll be ready for the Gigli saw in a sec.'

He showed her how to use the serrated wire saw, drawing a handle under the sternum with a pair of forceps and then joining the handles and using smooth, long strokes to cut through the sternum from the inside out.

Hannah was ready with the rib spreaders. For someone who hadn't done this before, her calmness and ability to follow direction was a huge bonus.

'You can see why this is called a "clam shell" thoracotomy,' he said as he spread the ribs away from the anterior incisions. 'Suction, thanks.'

Ryan sucked out blood and clots from the chest cavity, hoping it would be enough for the heart to start beating again spontaneously.

It wasn't.

'Where's she bleeding from?'

'Haven't found it yet.' Ryan placed both hands around the heart. 'I'm starting internal cardiac massage. Can you find and compress the aorta against the spine, Hannah? We want to maximise coronary and cerebral perfusion. I'll clamp it in a minute.'

She was totally out of her depth here. It was a huge relief when back-up from the cardiothoracic surgeons finally arrived. They were impressed with Ryan's management of the case so far, which was hardly surprising. Hannah wouldn't have had the confidence or skill to go further than the chest drain insertion.

The thought that Ryan might deserve the consultant's position more than she did was not a pleasant one.

Edged out as people with far more experience than she had took over, Hannah could only watch. It was hard, feeling the tension and increasing frustration as they failed to get the young woman's heart started again, having controlled the haemorrhage from the damaged aorta.

Maureen's signal, with the message that Brendon was now in the paediatric ICU and an invitation to discuss the results of the CT scan with the consultant, was welcome. Hannah slipped, unnoticed, from the resuscitation area.

She couldn't afford to stand around admiring Ryan's skill and thinking how easily he might win the position she'd wanted for so long. Or to share his disappointment at the inevitable failure he was facing. Empathy would create a connection that was too personal. Even worse than laughing at one of his stupid jokes. It would only make it that much harder to maintain the necessary distance between them.

Any reduction in that distance could only make her vulnerable.

And Hannah Jackson did not do vulnerable.

She'd always been the strong one. Ever since she was ten years old and her father's sudden death had made her small family almost fall apart. Hannah had been strong for her mother. For Susie. For herself.

The lesson had been hard but valuable. Strength was protection. The only way to get through life without being scarred too deeply.

Being too tired didn't help when it came to being strong.

When Hannah entered the staffroom nearly an hour later, she could feel Ryan's dejection all too easily. He had his back to her as he made coffee but his body language said it all. Slumped shoulders. Bent head. The way he was stirring his mug so slowly. If it had been any other colleague she wouldn't have hesitated in offering commiseration. A comforting touch or even a hug. But this was Ryan. Distance was obligatory.

'No go, huh?'

'Nah.' Ryan straightened his back. 'Didn't really expect to win that one but it was worth a try. Want coffee?'

'Sure, but I'll make it.'

Ryan was already spooning coffee into a second mug. 'You take sugar?'

'No.'

'Milk?'

'No.'

He'd been in the department for three months and didn't know how she took her coffee but she was willing to bet he'd know the preferences of all the female staff who responded to his flirting. And that was every one of them.

Except her.

'So how's your little guy, then?'

'Not flash. He's in paediatric ICU but the scan was horrible. Multi-focal bleeds. If he does survive, he'll be badly brain damaged.'

'Might be better if he doesn't, then. You saw the father?'

'Yeah.' There was no need for further comment. The glance Ryan gave Hannah as he handed her the mug of black coffee told her he shared her opinion that the man she'd had to talk to about the serious condition of his child was an uncaring brute. Responsible for the death of his wife and quite likely his son, not to mention the admittedly less serious injuries sustained by the other drivers involved, and he hadn't given the impression of being overly perturbed about any of it. 'And they can't even charge him for anything.'

'No.' Ryan went and sat down on one of the

comfortable armchairs dotted around the edge of the room.

The silence was heavy. Too heavy.

Ryan cleared his throat. 'Hey, have you heard the one about the blonde who didn't like blonde jokes?'

Hannah sighed. She sat down at the central table, deliberately putting Ryan out of sight behind her right shoulder. Maybe it wasn't good to sit in a depressed silence but this was going a bit too far in the other direction, wasn't it? She sipped her coffee without saying anything but Ryan clearly ignored the signals of disinterest.

'She went to this show where a ventriloquist was using his dummy to tell blonde jokes. You know, like, how do you change a blonde's mind?' He raised his voice and sounded as though he was trying to speak without moving his lips. "Blow in her ear!" And what do you do if a blonde throws a pin at you? "Run, she's still holding the grenade."'

'Yeah, yeah.' Hannah allowed herself to sound annoyed. 'I know.'

'Well, so did this blonde in the audience. She was furious. She jumps to her feet. "I've had enough of this", she shouts. "How dare you stereotype women this way? What does the colour of someone's hair have to do with her worth as a human being? It's people like you that keep women like me from reaching my full potential. You and your kind continue to perpetrate discrimination against not only blondes but women in general and it's *not* funny!"'

'Mmm.' Despite herself, Hannah was listening to the joke. So Ryan was actually aware of why someone like herself might take offence at his humour? Interesting. Did that mean he was intentionally trying to get under her skin? That his charm with her was as fake as it had been with Doris Matheson and he actually disliked her type as much as she did his?

Ryan's tone was deadpan. 'The ventriloquist was highly embarrassed. He goes red and starts apologising profusely but the blonde yells at him again. "Stay out of this, mister. I'm talking to that little jerk on your knee!"'

Hannah snorted. Somehow she managed to disguise the reluctant laughter as a sound more like derision. She didn't want to laugh, dammit! Not at one of Ryan's jokes and not when she'd just been through a gruelling, heart-breaking and probably fruitless couple of hours' work. She knew exactly why he was trying to make her laugh. It had to be the quickest way of defusing an overly emotional reaction to a case. But if she let him make her feel better, it would be worse than empathising with *him*. She could feel the connection there, waiting to happen. It needed dealing with. She had to push Ryan as far away as possible.

'You just can't help yourself, can you?'

'I thought you might appreciate that one.'

'What makes you think I'm in the mood for jokes right now?' Hannah swivelled so that she could give Ryan a direct look. 'Doesn't anything dent your warped sense of humour? Even a battered wife who died trying to get her child to a safe place?'

'That's precisely why I thought a joke might be a good idea,' Ryan said wearily. 'Sorry, maybe I should have left you to wallow in how awful it was. Maybe question your abilities and wonder endlessly what you might have been able to do better.'

'It might be more appropriate than telling jokes.'

'Really? What if another major case comes in in the next five minutes, Hannah? You going to be in a fit state to give that person the best you can?'

'Of course I am.'

'Well, lucky you. Some of us need to distract ourselves. Lift our spirits a bit. There's always time for wallowing later.'

'I don't believe you ever wallow,' Hannah snapped. She wasn't going to admit that even that stifled snort of laughter *had* done something to ease the emotional downside of this job. She'd rather believe that it was being able to channel her frustration and anger into a confrontation that had been building for some time. 'And you distract yourself often enough to be a liability in this department. You've been here, what, three months? And how many times have you taken time off to flit back to Australia? Four, five times? I should know—it's usually me that does extra shifts to cover the gaps.'

This distraction was working wonderfully well. Hannah was really hitting her stride.

'You know your problem, Ryan? You're shallow. You're so intent on having a fun life you can't even spare the time to think about someone else.'

'Oh?' Ryan was staring at Hannah and she'd never heard him use such an icy tone. 'Shallow, am I?'

'You might find it more beneficial to your career to review cases like we've just had. You never know. Try having a professional discussion with a colleague next time instead of telling *stupid* jokes. You might learn something.'

'From you?' Ryan snorted. 'I doubt it.'

'Why?' Hannah's tone was waspish. 'Because I'm blonde?'

'No.' Ryan stood up, abandoning his cup of coffee. 'Because you're less experienced professionally and far less competent when it comes to relationships between people. You're judgmental, Dr Jackson, and you don't even bother finding out the facts before you make those judgments.'

He stalked behind Hannah and she had to swivel her head to keep glaring at him as he made his parting shot. 'And when I'm consultant, it might be nice if you made *me* coffee, babe. Not the other way round.'

'Dream on, mate!' What a pathetic rejoinder.

Hannah could only hope Ryan would take it as she meant it—referring to the consultancy position and not the coffee-making.

Jennifer came in a few seconds after Ryan had left. Her eyebrows had disappeared under her fringe.

'What on earth's wrong with Ryan? I've never seen him look so grumpy!'

'He's a grumpy man.'

Jennifer laughed. 'He is not and you know it. He's a lovely man and if you weren't trying so hard not to like him you would have realised that by now.'

'I'm not trying hard,' Hannah protested. 'It's easy. Besides, it was your friend in Sydney that told you what a reputation he had for breaking hearts. The man needs an emotional health warning attached.'

Jennifer shook her head, smiling. 'Yeah... right.' She took another glance at Hannah. 'You look pretty grumpy yourself.'

'It's been a bad night. I hate cases like that—especially when they shouldn't have happened in the first place.' She sighed again. 'And I'm tired. Roll on 7 a.m.'

'Roll on Friday more like. Isn't that when you leave for a few days' R & R in the sun?'

'Sure is.' Hannah's spirits finally lifted—a lot more than Ryan's joke had achieved. 'You know, I'm finally really looking forward to this trip.'

'I could do with some time away from this place myself. Could be just what the doctor ordered. For both of us.'

'Mmm.' Hannah's agreement was whole-hearted. But it wasn't the place she needed the break from. A few days away from Ryan Fisher was definitely what this doctor was ordering.

Hannah Jackson could go to hell in a hand basket.

The glimpse of a woman with sleek blonde hair disappearing into the melee of economy class was enough of a reminder to sink Ryan Fisher's spirits with a nasty jolt.

He slid his cabin baggage into the overhead locker with the same ease he slid his long body into the comfortable window seat at the rear of the business class section of the plane. Seconds later, he returned the smile of a very pretty young air hostess.

'Orange juice would be lovely,' he agreed. 'Exactly what I need.'

The frosted glass was presented while economy-class passengers were still filing past, but Ryan killed the faintly embarrassed reaction to the envious glances. Why shouldn't he travel in comfort? He had to do it often enough to make it a boring inconvenience and he'd decided he may as well make the travel as enjoyable as possible when the destination usually wasn't.

At least this time he could look forward to what lay at the other end of his journey.

'Is there anything else you need, sir?'

Ryan suppressed a wry smile along with the temptation to ask the crew member for a thousand things. How about a miraculous cure for a little girl in Brisbane that he had far more than just a bond of family with? Or perhaps freedom from the ridiculously powerful attraction he had felt for Hannah Jackson ever since he'd first laid eyes on her three months ago?

No. He was over that. As of last Monday night when she'd told him exactly what she thought of him. She hated him. He was shallow—telling jokes when he should be taking on board the misery of others. Lazy—taking time off to flit back to Australia to have fun at regular intervals. Out to win the job she felt was rightfully hers.

Ironic that he'd actually set out to catch Hannah's attention by demonstrating his clinical ability. He hadn't expected the head of department to twist his arm and put his name forward for the upcoming consultancy position but then he'd thought, Why not? The anchor of a permanent job could be just what he needed to sort out his life. And at least that way Hannah would see him as an equal.

Would really *see* him.

How idiotic would it be to waste any more time or emotional energy hankering after someone who didn't even have any respect, let alone liking, for him?

'No, thanks.' He smiled. 'I'm fine.'

Ryan sipped his chilled juice, stretching his legs into the generous space in front of him and enjoying the fact that the seat beside him was empty. So were both the seats on the opposite side of the aisle. There was, in fact, only one other occupant of business class and Ryan found himself listening to the well-dressed man with an

American accent telling the air hostess that all he wanted was to go to sleep and could he have one of those eye covers? Apparently he hadn't expected a diversion to Auckland or a night in an airport hotel and he'd had more than enough of travelling for now.

'It should have been a straightforward trip to Sydney and then Cairns,' he was saying. 'Instead, I'm bunny-hopping through the south Pacific. Inefficient, that's what it is.'

'There's been a few disruptions due to some bad weather,' the hostess responded. 'Hopefully we'll be able to bypass it on this trip.'

Ryan didn't care if they hit a few bumps. Despite what Hannah thought of him, he didn't often get a smooth ride through life. OK, so maybe he didn't wear his heart on his sleeve and go around telling everyone his problems, but it was just as well, wasn't it? Imagine how low he'd be feeling right now if he'd made it obvious just how attracted he'd been to Hannah and had been squashed like the bug she clearly thought he was?

Well, she wouldn't get the opportunity now. No way. He wouldn't have her if she threw herself at him. Wrapped up in a ribbon and nothing else.

A soft sound like a strangled groan escaped. That short flight into fantasy wasn't likely to help anything. He drained his glass and handed it back as part of the preparation for take-off. Then he closed his eyes as the big jet rolled towards the end of the runway. Maybe he should follow the example of the other occupant of business class and escape into a few hours of peaceful oblivion.

The trip promised to be anything but restful. Hannah had an aisle seat, for which she was becoming increasingly grateful. It meant she could lean outwards.

She had to lean outwards because the man beside her was one of the fattest people Hannah had ever seen. He could easily have used up two seats all by himself but somehow he had squeezed in. Apart from the parts of his body that oozed through the gaps above and below the armrests and encroached considerably on Hannah's space. Any sympathy for his obvious discomfort had been replaced by a more selfish concern about her own when the personality of her travelling companion began to reveal itself.

'Name's Blair,' he boomed at her. 'How's it going?' He certainly wasn't shy. 'They make these seats a bit bloody small these days, eh? Just want to pack us in like sardines so they make a profit.'

'Mmm.' And they were allocated the same amount of baggage weight, Hannah thought crossly. What would happen if every passenger was Blair's size? Could the plane flip over because the baggage compartment was too light? Use twice as much fuel? Drop out of the sky?

Hannah wasn't a great fan of flying. She leaned further into the aisle and gripped the armrest on that side as the plane gathered speed.

'Not keen on flying, huh?' Blair was leaning, too. 'Wanna hold my hand?'

'Ah…no, thanks.' Hannah screwed her eyes shut. 'I'm just fine.'

'It's OK. ' Blair was laughing as the wheels left the tarmac. 'I'm single.'

There was no point pretending to be asleep because Blair didn't seem to notice. He obviously liked to think aloud and kept himself amused by a running commentary on the choice of movies available, the tourist attractions of Cairns showcased in the airline magazine and the length of time it was taking for the cabin crew to start serving refreshments.

The reason for any delay was revealed when the captain's voice sounded in the cabin.

'G'day, folks. Welcome aboard this Air New Zealand flight to Cairns. We're expecting a bit of turbulence due to strong westerly winds courtesy of a tropical cyclone in the Coral Sea region going by the name of Willie. I'm going to keep the crew seated until we get through this next layer of cloud.'

Blair made a grumbling sound.

'Once we're cruising at around thirty-five thousand feet, things should get a bit smoother,' the captain continued. 'You'll be free to move around the cabin at that point but I would suggest that while you're in your seats you do keep your seat belts firmly fastened.'

Sure enough, the flight became smoother and the cabin crew began to serve drinks and meals. The steward that stopped beside Hannah cast a second glance at her companion, listened to him patiently while he complained about the delay in being fed and then winked at Hannah.

'I'll be back in a tick,' he said.

When he returned, he bent down and whispered in Hannah's ear. Then he opened the overhead locker and removed the bag she specified. Hannah unclipped her seat belt and stood up with a sigh of relief.

'Hey!' Blair was watching the removal of the bag with concern. 'Where're you going, darling?'

'We've got a bit of room up front,' the steward informed him. 'I'm just juggling passengers a bit. If you lift the armrest there, Sir, I'm sure you'll find the journey a lot more comfortable.'

Much to Hannah's astonishment, 'up front' turned out to be an upgrade to business class. Her eyes widened as she realised she was going to have a window seat—no, both the seats—all to herself.

'You're an angel of mercy,' she told the steward. 'Wow! I've never flown business class before.'

'Enjoy!' The steward grinned. 'I'll make sure they bring you something to drink while you settle in and have a look at the breakfast menu.'

Hannah sank into the soft seat, unable to contain her smile. She stretched out her legs and wiggled her toes. Not much chance of developing a DVT here. There was any amount of elbow room, as well. She tested it, sticking her arms out like wings. She even flapped them up and down a little. Just as well there was no one to see her doing a duck impression.

Or was there? Hannah hadn't yet considered the possibility of a passenger on the other side of the aisle. She turned her head swiftly, aware of a blush starting. And then she recognised the solitary figure by the window and she actually gasped aloud.

Glaring was probably the only description she could have used for the way Ryan Fisher was looking at her.

'Oh, my God!' Hannah said. 'What are *you* doing here?'

CHAPTER THREE

'I WAS about to ask you the same thing.'

'I got upgraded.' Hannah hadn't intended to sound defensive. Why did this man always bring out the worst in her? 'Things were a bit crowded down the back.'

'Here you go, Dr Jackson.' A pretty, redheaded hostess held out a tray with a fluted glass on it. 'And here's the menu. I'll come back in a minute to see what you'd like for breakfast.'

'Thank you.' Hannah took a sip of her juice and pretended to study the menu, which gave a surprisingly wide choice for the first meal of the day. There were hours of this flight left. Was she going to have to make conversation with Ryan the whole way?

It was some sort of divine retribution. Hannah had been feeling guilty ever since Monday night

when she'd let fly and been so rude to a colleague. She couldn't blame him for either the re-
taliation or the way he'd been avoiding her for
the last few days. The personal attack had been
unprofessional and probably undeserved. He
couldn't know where the motivation had come
from and Hannah certainly couldn't tell him
but…maybe she ought to apologise?

She flicked a quick glance from the menu
towards Ryan. He was still glaring. He wasn't
about to use their first meeting away from work
to try building any bridges, was he?

Hannah wished she hadn't looked. Hadn't
caught those dark eyes. She couldn't open her
mouth to say anything because goodness only
knew what might shoot out, given the peculiar
situation of being in this man's company away
from a professional setting. Imagine if she
started and then couldn't stop?

If she told him her whole life history? About
the man her mother had really fallen in love
with—finally happy after years of getting over
her husband's tragic death. Of the way she'd
been used and then abandoned. Hannah had
known not to trust the next one that had come

along. Why hadn't her mother been able to see through him that easily? Perhaps the attraction to men like that was genetic and too powerful to resist. It might explain why Susie had made the same mistake. Fortunately, Hannah was stronger. She might *want* Ryan Fisher but there was no way she would allow herself to *have* him.

Oddly, the satisfying effect of pushing him firmly out of her emotional orbit the other night was wearing off. Here she was contemplating an apology. An attempt at establishing some kind of friendship even.

Ryan hadn't blinked.

Hannah realised this in the same instant she realised she could only have noticed because she hadn't looked away. The eye contact had continued for too long and…Oh, *God!* What if Ryan had seen even a fraction of what she'd been thinking?

Attack was the best form of defence, wasn't it?

'Why are you staring at me?'

'I'm still waiting for you to answer my question.'

'What question?'

'What you're doing here.'

'I told you, I got upgraded.'

'You know perfectly well that wasn't what I meant. What the hell are you doing on this flight?'

'Going to Cairns.' Hannah didn't need the change in Ryan's expression to remind her how immature it was to be so deliberately obtuse. She gave in. 'I've got a connecting flight at Cairns to go to a small town further north in Queensland. Crocodile Creek.'

Lips that were usually in some kind of motion, either talking or smiling, went curiously slack. The tone of Ryan's voice was also stunned.

'You're going to *Crocodile Creek?*'

'Yes.'

'So am I.'

'Did you decide what you'd like for breakfast, Dr Jackson?'

'What?' Hannah hadn't even noticed the approach of the redheaded stewardess. 'Oh, sorry. Um… Anything's fine. I'm starving!'

The stewardess smiled. 'I'll see what I can surprise you with.' She turned to the other side of the aisle. 'And you, Dr Fisher? Have you decided?'

'I'll have the fresh fruit salad and a mushroom omelette, thanks.'

Ryan didn't want to be surprised by his breakfast. Maybe he'd just had enough of a surprise. As had Hannah. She waited only a heartbeat after the stewardess had moved away.

'Is there a particular reason why you're going to Crocodile Creek at this particular time?''

'Sure is. I'm best man at my best mate's wedding.'

'Oh…' Hannah swallowed carefully. 'That would be…Mike?'

Ryan actually closed his eyes. 'And you know that because you're also invited to the wedding?'

'Yes.'

Ryan made a sound like a chuckle but it was so unlike the laughter Hannah would have recognised she wasn't sure it had anything to do with amusement. 'Don't tell me you're lined up to be the bridesmaid.'

'No, of course I'm not. I don't know Emily that well.'

'Thank God for that.'

'My sister's the bridesmaid.'

Ryan's eyes opened smartly. Hannah could have sworn she saw something like a flash of fear. Far more likely to be horror, she decided. He disliked her so much that the prospect of being a partner to her sister was appalling? That hurt. Hannah couldn't resist retaliating.

'My twin sister,' she said. She smiled at Ryan. 'We're identical.'

Ryan shook his head. 'I don't believe this.'

'It is a bit of a coincidence,' Hannah agreed, more cheerfully. Ryan was so disconcerted that she actually felt like she had control of this situation—an emotional upper hand—and that had to be a first for any time she had spent in Ryan's company, with the exception of Monday night. Maybe this wouldn't be so bad after all. 'So, how come you know Mike so well?'

But Ryan didn't appear to be listening. 'There are two of you,' he muttered. 'Unbelievable!'

Their conversation was interrupted by the arrival of their food. Hannah was hungry enough to get stuck into the delicious hot croissants and jam she was served. Ryan was only halfway through his fruit salad by the time she had cleaned her plate and he didn't look as though he was particularly enjoying the start of his meal.

Hannah had to feel sorry for him but she

couldn't resist teasing just a little. She adopted the same, slightly aggrieved tone he had been using only a short time ago.

'You didn't answer my question.'

'What question?' Ryan wasn't being deliberately obtuse. He looked genuinely bewildered.

'How do you know Mike? The groom at this wedding we're both going to.'

'Oh… I was involved in training paramedics in the armed forces for a while, years ago. Mike was keen to add medical training to his qualifications as a helicopter pilot, having been in a few dodgy situations. We hit it off and have stayed in touch ever since.' Ryan stirred the contents of his bowl with the spoon. 'I was really looking forward to seeing him again,' he added sadly. 'The last real time we had together was a surfing holiday in Bali nearly three years ago. After he got out of the army but before he took himself off to the back of beyond.'

'Crocodile Creek does seem a bit out of the way,' Hannah had to agree. Besides, thinking about geography was a good way to distract herself from feeling offended that Ryan seemed to think all the pleasure might have been sucked from the upcoming weekend. 'It was easy enough to hop on a plane to Brisbane to spend a day or two with Susie.'

'I got the impression you never took time off.'

'I don't take rostered time off.'

'Unlike me.' Ryan said it for her. ''Cos you're not lazy.'

Hannah wasn't going to let this conversation degenerate into a personality clash. Here was the opportunity she had needed. 'I never said you were lazy, Ryan. You work as hard as I do. You're just more inclined to take time off.'

'For the purposes of having fun.'

'Well…yes…' Hannah shrugged. 'And why not?' Would this count as an apology, perhaps? 'All work and no play, etcetera.'

'Makes Jack a dull boy,' Ryan finished. 'And Jill a very dull girl.'

Was he telling Hannah she was dull? Just a more pointed comment than Jennifer telling her she was an ED geek? If he saw her as being more *fun*—say at a wedding reception—would he find her more attractive?

Hannah stomped on the wayward thought. She

didn't want Ryan to find her attractive. She didn't want to find *him* attractive, for heaven's sake! It was something that had just happened. Like a lightning bolt. A bit of freak weather—like the cyclone currently brewing in the Coral Sea, which was again causing a bit of turbulence for the jet heading for Cairns.

The two cabin-crew members pushing a meal trolley through to economy class exchanged a doubtful glance.

'Should we wait a bit before serving the back section?'

'No.' The steward who had been responsible for Hannah's upgrade shook his head. 'Let's get it done, then we can clear up. If we're going to hit any really rough stuff, it'll be when we're north of Brisbane.'

Hannah tightened her seat belt a little.

'Nervous?' Ryan must have been watching her quite closely to observe the action.

'I'm not that keen on turbulence.'

'Doesn't bother me.' Ryan smiled at Hannah. Or had that smile been intended for the approaching stewardess? 'I quite like a bumpy ride.'

Hannah and Ryan both chose coffee rather than tea. Of course the smile had been for the pretty redhead. Likewise the comment that could easily have been taken as blatant flirting.

'I don't know Emily,' Ryan said. 'Maybe you can fill me in. She's a doctor, yes?'

'Yes. She's Susie's best friend.'

'Susie?'

'My sister.'

'The clone. Right. So how long has she been in Crocodile Creek?'

'About three years. She went to Brisbane to get some post-grad training after she finished her physiotherapy degree and she liked it so much she decided to stay.'

'I thought she was a doctor.'

'No. She started medical school with me but it wasn't what she wanted.'

'How come she lives in that doctors' house that used to be the old hospital, then?'

'She doesn't.'

'That's not what Mike told me.'

'Why would Mike be telling you about my sister?'

'He wasn't. He was telling me about his

fiancée. Emily.' Ryan groaned. 'We're not on the same page here, are we?'

'No.' And they never would be. 'Sorry. I don't know much about Emily either, except that she's a really nice person and totally in love with Mike and his parents are thrilled and hoping for lots of grandchildren.'

Ryan was still frowning. 'If you don't know Emily and you don't know Mike, why have you been invited to their wedding?'

'As Susie's partner, kind of. We haven't seen each other since Christmas.'

'That's not so long ago.'

Hannah shrugged. 'It seems a long time. We're close, I guess.'

'Hmm.'

Ryan's thoughts may as well have been in a bubble over his head. As best man, he would have to partner Hannah's clone. Another woman who wouldn't be on the same page. Someone else who would think he was shallow and lazy and a liability.

Hannah opened her mouth to offer some reassurance. To finally apologise for losing it on Monday night in such an unprofessional manner.

To suggest that they would both be able to have a good time at the wedding despite having each other's company enforced.

She didn't get the chance.

Her mouth opened far more widely than needed for speech as the plane hit an air pocket and seemed to drop like a rock. The fall continued long enough for someone further down the plane in economy to scream, and then they got to the bottom with a crunch and all hell broke loose.

The big jet slewed sideways into severe turbulence. The pitch of its engine roar increased. The water glass and cutlery on Hannah's tray slithered sideways to clatter to the floor. The seat-belt sign on the overhead panel flashed on and off repeatedly with a loud dinging noise. Oxygen masks were deployed and swung like bizarre, short pendulums. Children were shrieking and someone was calling for help. The stewardess who had been pushing the meal trolley staggered through the curtain dividing business class from the rest of the cabin, her face covered in blood. She fell into the seat beside Hannah.

'I can't see anything!'

Hannah was still clutching her linen napkin in

her hand. She pushed the tray table up and latched it, giving her space to turn to the woman beside her, who was trying to wipe the blood from her eyes.

'Hold still!' Hannah instructed. She folded the napkin into a rough pad. If her years of training and practice in emergency departments had done nothing else, Hannah would always bless the ability to focus on an emergency without going to pieces herself. 'You've got a nasty cut on your forehead.' She pressed the pad against the wound as best she could, with the plane continuing to pitch and roll.

'I came down on the corner of the trolley.'

'What's happening?' Ryan was out of his seat, hanging onto an armrest for support.

By way of answer, calmly overriding the noise of the engines and distressed passengers, came the voice from the flight deck.

'Sorry about this, folks. Bit of unexpected rough stuff. We should be through this pretty fast. Please, return to your seats and keep your belts firmly fastened for the moment.'

Ryan ignored the direction. 'Anyone else hurt back there?'

'I don't know.' The stewardess was leaning back in the seat, her face pale beneath smeared blood. 'We were still serving breakfast. It'll be a mess. I should go and help.'

Ryan held back the curtain to look into the main body of the cabin. Clearly, he was trying to see where he might be needed most urgently. Forgetting one's own fear and helping someone who'd happened to land in the seat beside her was nothing compared to the courage it would need to take command of the kind of chaos Hannah could imagine Ryan assessing.

Mixed in with her admiration of his intention was a desire to prove she could also rise to the occasion. Ryan's courage was contagious.

'Hold this.' Hannah took the hand of the stewardess and placed it over the pad. 'Keep firm pressure on it and the bleeding will stop soon. I'll come back and check on you in a bit.' She unclipped her seat belt and stood up. The oxygen mask bumped her head but Hannah ignored it. The jolt from the air pocket must have caused their deployment because she wasn't at all short of breath so the oxygen level had to be OK. Lurching sideways to get past the knees of the stewardess, Hannah found her arm firmly gripped by Ryan.

'What *do* you think you're doing, Hannah? Sit down and belt up.'

'Help!' A male voice was yelling loudly. 'We need a doctor!'

'Stay here,' Ryan ordered crisply. 'I'll go.'

But Hannah knew that her own courage was coming from the confidence Ryan was displaying. If he left, she might be tempted to strap herself safely back into her seat and wait for the turbulence to end.

People needed help.

'No,' she said. 'I'm coming with you.'

Something unusual showed in Ryan's eyes. Did he know how terrified she was? What an effort trying to match his bravery was?

Maybe he did. The glance felt curiously like applause. He let go of her arm and took her hand instead, to lead her through the curtain. Hannah found herself gripping his fingers. He'd only done it to save her falling if there was more turbulence, but she was going to allow herself to take whatever she needed from this physical connection. What did it matter, when it felt like they might all be going to plunge to their deaths at any moment?

She followed Ryan through the curtain to become the new focus for dozens of terrified passengers as they moved down the aisle. Some were wearing their oxygen masks, others trying to get them on. She saw a young woman with her face in her hands, sobbing. A much older woman, nursing what looked like a fractured wrist. A nun, clutching her crucifix, her lips moving in silent prayer. The steward was waving at them from the rear of the aircraft.

'Here! Help!' he shouted. 'I think this man's choking.'

'It's Blair!' Hannah exclaimed.

Her former seat neighbour was standing, blocking the aisle. His hand was around his neck in the universal signal of distress from choking and his face was a dreadful, mottled purple.

Ryan was moving fast. He let go of Hannah's hand to climb over the empty seat that had initially been hers to get behind Blair.

'I've tried banging him on the back,' the steward said unhappily.

Ryan put his arms around Blair but couldn't

grasp his fist with his other hand to perform an effective Heimlich manoeuvre. There was just too much of Blair to encompass and there was no time. The huge man was rapidly losing consciousness and there was no way Ryan could support his weight unaided.

Blair slumped onto his back, blocking the aisle even more effectively. There was no way for anyone to move. Ryan looked up and Hannah could see he was aware of how impossible it was going to be to try and manage this emergency. She could also see that he had no intention of admitting defeat. It was a very momentary impression, however, because the plane hit another bump and Hannah went hurtling forward to land in a most undignified fashion directly on top of Blair.

She landed hard and then used her hands on his chest to push herself upright. Blair gave a convulsive movement beneath her and Hannah slid her legs in front of her old empty seat to try and slide clear. Ryan grabbed Blair's shoulder and heaved and suddenly Blair was on his side, coughing and spluttering. Ryan thumped him hard between his shoulder blades for good measure and the crisis was over, probably as quickly as it had begun, as Blair forcibly spat out what looked like a large section of a sausage.

'Let's sit you up,' Ryan said firmly.

Blair was still gasping for air and had tears streaming down his face but somehow, with the help of the steward and another passenger, they got him back into his seat. Hannah jerked the oxygen mask down to start the flow. At least one person was going to benefit from their unnecessary deployment.

'We're through the worst of it now, folks. Should be plain sailing from now on.'

The timing of the captain's message was enough to make Hannah smile wryly. Catching Ryan's gaze, her smile widened.

'He doesn't know how right he is, does he?'

Ryan grinned right back at her, with the kind of killer smile he gave to so many women. The kind that old Doris Matheson had received the other night. But it was the first time Hannah had felt the full force of it and for just a fraction of a second it felt like they had connected.

Really connected. More than that imaginary connection Hannah had taken from the hand-holding.

And it felt astonishingly good.

Good enough to carry Hannah through the next hour of helping to treat the minor injuries sustained. Splinting the Colles' fracture on the old woman's wrist, bandaging lacerations and examining bruises.

The other occupant of business class had been woken by the turbulence and offered his services.

'I'm a neurosurgeon,' he said. 'Name's Alistair Carmichael. What can I do to help?'

'We've got a stewardess with a forehead laceration,' Hannah told him. 'You're the perfect person to check and make sure she's not showing any signs of concussion—or worse. Mostly, I think it's going to be a matter of reassuring people.'

Hannah made more than one stop to check that Blair wasn't suffering any lingering respiratory distress.

Ryan worked just as hard. The first-aid supplies on the plane were rapidly depleted but it didn't matter. The plane was making a smooth descent into Cairns and Blair, who had been the closest to a fatal injury, was beaming.

'You saved my life, darling,' he told Hannah when he was helped from the plane at Cairns by paramedics who would take him to hospital for a thorough check-up.

'Yes.' Ryan's voice seemed to be coming from somewhere very close to Hannah's ear and she gave an involuntary shiver. 'Interesting technique, that. You should write it up for a medical journal.'

Hannah turned her head. Was he making fun of her?

'The "Jackson manoeuvre",' Ryan said with a grin.

Hannah was too tired to care whether he was laughing at her. And the incident *had* had a very funny side. 'Yeah,' she said. 'Or maybe the "Blonde's Heimlich"?'

Much to Ryan's disappointment, they weren't sitting anywhere near each other on the connecting flight to Crocodile Creek, despite the much smaller size of the aircraft. It seemed to have been taken over by a large contingent of rather excited Greek people who had to be part of Mike's family. They were too busy talking and arguing with each other to take notice of strangers, and that suited Ryan just fine. He was tired and felt like he had too much to think about anyway.

Fancy Hannah being able to laugh at herself like that! Or had it been some kind of dig at him? Ryan knew perfectly well how his blonde jokes got up her nose. They had become a kind of defence mechanism so that no one would guess how disappointed he was when Hannah took no notice of him. He might get a negative reaction to the jokes but at least she knew he existed.

And what about the way she hadn't hesitated to go and help others when she had clearly been terrified herself by the turbulence. That had taken a lot of courage. She obviously didn't like flying. Ryan had seen the way she'd looked at the size of their connecting aircraft. He hoped she was as reassured as he had been by the information that the tropical storm was now moving out to sea and their next journey would be much smoother. They were even forecasting relatively fine weather for the rest of the day.

'But make the most of it,' the captain warned. 'It could turn nasty again tomorrow.'

That caused the volume of conversation around him to increase dramatically as the Greek wedding guests discussed the ramifications of bad weather. Ryan tuned out of what sounded like superstitious babble of how to overcome such a bad omen.

Hannah was sitting as far away as it was possible to be down the back of the cabin. Had she arranged that somehow? She was beside the American neurosurgeon, Alistair, who had proved himself to be a very pleasant and competent man during the aftermath of the turbulence. Distinctive looking, too, with those silver streaks in his dark hair. He had put the jacket of his pinstriped suit back on but he was asleep again.

There was an odd relief in noticing that. Surely any other man would find Hannah as attractive as he did? And he hadn't known the half of it, had he? No wonder he hadn't recognised her from behind on the larger plane. He'd only seen her with her sleek blonde hair wound up in a kind of knot thing and baggy scrubs covering her body. The tight-fitting jeans and soft white shirt she was wearing today revealed a shape as perfect as her face.

Impossible to resist the urge to crane his neck once more and check that the American was still asleep. He was. So was Hannah, which was just as well. Ryan wouldn't want her to know he'd stolen another glance. He settled back and dozed himself and it seemed no time until the wheels touched down on a much smaller runway than the last one.

He was here. At the back of beyond, in Crocodile Creek. For three whole days. With Hannah Jackson. What had happened to that fierce resolve with which he had started this journey? That Hannah could go to hell because he was no longer interested? That he was completely over that insane attraction?

It had been shaken by that turbulence, that's what. It had gone out the window when he'd taken hold of her hand and she hadn't pulled away. Had—amazingly—held his hand right back.

Ryan sighed deeply and muttered inaudibly.

'Let the fun begin.'

CHAPTER FOUR

HEAT hit her like a blast from a furnace door swinging open.

Thanks to the early departure from Auckland and the time difference between Australia and New Zealand, it was the hottest part of the day when they arrived in Crocodile Creek.

The bad weather that had made the first leg of the journey so memorable seemed to have been left well behind. The sky was an intense, cobalt blue and there were no clouds to filter the strength of the sun beating down. It was hot.

Very hot.

Descending the steps from the back of the small plane onto the shimmering tarmac, Hannah realised what a mistake it had been to travel in jeans.

'I'm cooking!' She told Susie by way of a

greeting as she entered the small terminal building. 'How hot *is* it?'

'Must be nearly forty degrees.' Susie was hugging Hannah hard. 'What on earth possessed you to wear jeans?' She was far more sensibly dressed, in shorts, a singlet top and flip-flop sandals.

'It was cold when I got up at stupid o'clock. Our flight left at 6 a.m.' Hannah pulled back from the hug. 'You've let your hair grow. It looks fabulous.'

Susie dragged her fingers through her almost shoulder-length golden curls. 'It'd be as long as yours now, if I bothered straightening it.'

'Don't!' Hannah said in mock alarm. 'If you did that, nobody would be able to tell us apart and it would be school all over again.'

'Yeah…' Susie was grinning. 'With you getting into trouble for the things I did.'

The noise in the small building increased markedly as the main group of passengers entered, to be greeted ecstatically by the people waiting to meet them. The loud voices, tears and laughter and exuberant hugging made Susie widen her eyes.

'That's *another* Poulos contingent arriving. Look at that! This wedding is a circus.'

Why did Hannah's gaze seek Ryan out in the crowd so instantly? As though the smallest excuse made it permissible? She turned back to Susie.

'What's your bridesmaid's dress like?'

'Pink.'

'Oh, my God, you're *kidding!*'

'Yeah. It's peach but it's still over the top. Sort of a semi-meringue. Kind of like you'd expect some finalist in a ballroom dancing competition to be wearing. I could keep it to get married in myself eventually—except for the lack of originality. Five other girls will have the same outfit at home.'

'*Six* bridesmaids?'

'Yes, but I'm the most important one. Poor Emily doesn't have any family and she only wanted two bridesmaids—me and Mike's sister, Maria, but there were all these cousins who would have been mortally offended if they hadn't been included and, besides, Mike's mum, Sophia, is determined to have the wedding of the century. I think she only stopped at six because it was getting hard to find the male counterparts. Funnily enough, they weren't so keen.'

'How's Emily holding up?'

'She's loving every minute of it but going absolutely mad. And she'll need a lot of make-up tomorrow to cover red cheeks from all the affectionate pinching she's getting.' Susie's head was still turning as she scanned the rest of the arrivals. 'Let's go and find your bag before we get swamped. If Sophia starts introducing me as the chief bridesmaid, I'll probably get *my* cheeks pinched as well. Oh, my God!' Susie did a double take as she lowered her voice. 'Who is *that?*'

There were two men standing a little to one side of the crowd, their attention on the signs directing them to the baggage collection area. One of them was Ryan. His head started to turn as though he sensed Hannah's gaze so she transferred it quickly to the other man. It was easy to recognise the person who had been dozing in the seat beside her on the last leg of her long journey. In that suit, he had to be even hotter than Hannah was in her jeans.

'He's an American,' she told Susie. 'A neurosurgeon. Alistair…someone. He's here for the wedding but he didn't say much about it. I got the impression he wasn't that thrilled to be coming.'

'That's Gina's cousin, then. Gorgeous, isn't he?'

'I guess.' Hannah hadn't taken much notice. Who would, when someone that looked like Ryan Fisher was nearby? 'Gina?'

'Also American. A cardiologist. She's getting married to Cal next weekend. I told you all about her at Christmas. She arrived with her little boy, who turned out to be Cal's son. Cal's one of our surgeons.'

'Right. Whew! *Two* weddings in two weeks?'

'Wedding city,' Susie agreed. She was leading the way past where the men were standing. Hannah could feel the odd prickle on the back of her neck that came when you knew someone was watching you. She didn't turn around because it was unlikely that she'd feel the stare of someone she didn't know with such spine-tingling clarity.

'Some people are going to both weddings,' Susie continued, ' and they've had to travel to get here so everybody thought they might like to just stay and have a bit of a holiday in between.'

'He won't have much of a holiday if he stays in that suit. And I thought I was overdressed!'

'Oh! The guy in the suit is the American?'

Susie threw a glance over her shoulder. 'So who's the really gorgeous one who's staring at you?'

Hannah sighed. 'That'll be Ryan.'

'Ryan Fisher? The best man?'

'Yes.'

'Wow!' Susie's grin widened. 'My day's looking up! Mike told me what a fabulous guy he is but he forgot to mention he was also fabulous looking.'

'Don't get too excited,' Hannah warned.

'Why? Is he married?'

'No, but he might not be too friendly.'

Susie's eyebrows vanished under the curls on her forehead. 'Why not?'

Hannah sighed inwardly, feeling far too hot and weary to start explaining why her sister could well have to deal with unreasonable antipathy from someone because he disliked her mirror image.

'I'll fill you in later.' It was much easier to change the subject. Very easy, in fact. 'Good grief!'

'What?' Susie's head turned to follow the direction of Hannah's astonished stare at the small, dark woman wearing black leather pants, a top that showed an amazing cleavage and...red stiletto shoes. 'That's Georgie.' She smiled. 'You'll meet her later.'

As though that explained everything! 'She must be as hot as hell in those clothes.'

'She's got super air-con for travel. She rides a Harley.'

'In *stilettos?*' Hannah's peripheral vision caught the way Ryan was also staring at the woman. There was no mistaking the appreciative grin on his face. 'Good *grief,*' she muttered again.

'I guess Georgie's here to meet Alistair. Georgie's Gina's bridesmaid and Alistair's here to give Gina away. He was supposed to arrive yesterday but his flight from the US was delayed by bad weather, and Gina and Cal are on one of the outer islands today, doing a clinic. So wow! Georgie and Alistair...' Susie shook her head. 'Leathers and pinstripes. They look a perfect couple. Not! Is that your bag?'

'Yes. Coming off first for a change.'

'Let's go, then.'

While it was a relief to escape the terminal building—and Ryan—it was a shock to step back out into the heat. And the wind. Huge fronds on the palm trees were bowing under its strength and Hannah had to catch her hair as it whipped into her face.

'Hurry up, Hannah! My car's over here and we're going to run out of time if we don't get going.'

'But the wedding's not till 4 p.m. tomorrow.' It was too hot to move any faster. 'What's the rush?' Hannah climbed reluctantly into the interior of a small hatchback car that felt more like an oven and immediately rolled down her window.

Susie started the engine and fiddled with the air-conditioning controls. 'It's all a bit frantic. I'm sorry. There's a rehearsal later this afternoon and I've got a couple more patients I just have to see before then.' She turned onto the main road and the car picked up speed rapidly. 'If you roll up your window, the air-con will work a lot better.'

Hannah complied and a welcome trickle of cool air came from the vents.

'Are you seeing your patients at your rooms?'

'No, I've finished the private stuff for today. These are hospital cases. Old Mrs Trengrove has had a hip replacement and absolutely refuses to get out of bed unless I'm there to hold her hand, and Wally's been admitted—he's one of my arthritis patients and it's his birthday today so I'll have to go and say hello.'

'Do you want to just drop me off at your place? I'm sure I could find my way to the beach and have a swim or something.'

'No, you can't swim at the beach. The water's all horrible because of the awful weather we've had in the last few days and it's stinger season. With the big waves we've been getting, the nets might not be working too well. Besides, I want to show you around the hospital. If you take your bathing suit, you could have a dip in the hospital pool.'

'Sounds good.' Hannah tried to summon enthusiasm for the busman's holiday delight of visiting the hospital.

'It's fabulous. You'd love it, Hannah. Hey…' Susie turned to look at her sister. 'They're always short of doctors. You could come and live with me for a while.'

'I couldn't stand working in heat like this.'

'It's not always like this.'

'It *is* beautiful.' Hannah was looking past

sugar-cane plantations and the river towards rainforest-covered mountains in the distance.

'Wait till you see the cove. You'll fall in love with it just like I did.'

'The roads are quieter than I expected.'

'Bit quieter than usual today. I expect it's got something to do with the big fishing competition that's on.'

They crossed the river that gave Crocodile Creek township its name, drove through the main part of town and then rattled over an old wooden bridge to cross the river again. Rounding the bend on a gentle downhill slope, Hannah got the postcard view. The picture-perfect little cove with the white sandy beach and the intriguing, smudged outlines of islands further out to sea.

'The sea's the wrong colour at the moment,' Susie said apologetically. 'It's usually as blue as the sky. That's the Athina.' She pointed at the sprawling white building with Greek-style lettering on its sign that advertised its function as a boutique hotel. 'That's where the reception is being held tomorrow. And that rambling, huge house on the other side of the cove is the doctors' house.'

'Ah! The original hospital which is now the hotbed of romance.'

'Don't knock it!' Susie grinned at her sister. 'You could live there if you didn't want to squeeze into my wee cottage. Who knows? You might just find the man of your dreams in residence.'

'Doubt it.'

'Yeah.' Susie chuckled. 'The man of *your* dreams is probably buried in a laboratory somewhere. Or a library. Or an accountant's office.'

'Dad was an accountant,' Hannah reminded her. 'It didn't stop him being a lot of fun.'

'True.' Susie was silent for a moment. 'And Trevor was a brain surgeon and had to be the most boring man I'd ever met.'

'Hey, you're talking about the man I was engaged to for three years.'

'And why did you break it off?'

Hannah laughed. 'Because I was bored to tears. OK, I agree. There should be a happy medium but I haven't found it yet.'

'Me neither,' Susie said sadly. 'There always turns out to be something wrong with them. Or, worse, they find something wrong with me.' She screwed up her nose as she turned towards her sister. 'What *is* wrong with me, Hannah?'

'Absolutely nothing,' Hannah said stoutly. 'The guys are just idiots and don't deserve you. You're gorgeous.'

'That makes you gorgeous as well, you realise.'

'Of course.' Hannah grinned.

This was what she missed most about not having Susie living nearby any more. The comfort of absolute trust. Knowing you could say anything—even blow your own trumpet— without having it taken the wrong way. Not that they didn't have the occasional row but nothing could damage the underlying bond. And nothing else ever came close to the kind of strength a bond like this could impart.

'We're both gorgeous,' she said. 'Smart, too.'

'I'm not as smart as you. You're a brilliant doctor, soon-to-be emergency medicine specialist. I'm only a physiotherapist.'

'You could have easily been a doctor if you'd wanted, as you well know, Susan Jackson. You're doing what you want to do and you're doing it brilliantly. Anyway, being seen as clever isn't an advantage when it comes to men. It intimidates them.'

Although Hannah had a feeling that Ryan Fisher would be stimulated rather than intimidated by an intelligent woman if he ever bothered trying to find out.

'Look!' Susie was distracted from the conversation now. 'That's the Black Cockatoo, our local. And that's Kylie's Klipz. Kylie's amazing—looks like Dolly Parton. She's our hairdresser and she'll be doing all the hair and make-up for tomorrow. That's the Grubbs' place with that rusty old truck parked on the lawn and…here's my place.'

Susie parked outside a tiny cottage with two front windows in the shade of a veranda that was almost invisible beneath bougainvillea.

'Cute!'

'Speaking of cute.' Susie was unlocking her front door as Hannah carried her bag from the car. 'What's wrong with Ryan Fisher? Was he rude to you on the plane or something?'

'Not exactly. I just happen to know he's a player.'

'How do you know that? Do you know someone that works with him in Sydney?'

'He doesn't work in Sydney any more. He works in Auckland.'

'As in the same place you work?' Susie had opened the door but hadn't made any move to go inside.

'Exactly.'

'He's in your ED?'

'He's the guy who's after my job. I told you about him.'

Susie's jaw dropped. '*Ryan's* the holiday king? The Aussie playboy who's been driving you nuts with all those blonde jokes?'

'That's him.'

'The one who's out to date every nurse in the department in record time?'

'Yep.'

'So why have you been calling him Richard the third in your emails?'

'Because he reminds me of that bastard that Mum fell in love with when she'd finally got over Dad's death. *And* the creep who dumped you just before you went to Brisbane. He's a certain type. Skitters through life having a good time and not worrying about hurting anyone along the way. A flirt.'

'I'll bet he doesn't have any trouble getting a response.'

'He drives a flashy car. A BMW Roadster or something.'

'Nice. Soft top?'

Hannah ignored the teasing. 'He knows I can see right through the image. He hates *me*, too.'

Susie finally moved, leading the way into one of the bedrooms at the front of the cottage. 'I didn't get that impression from the way he was staring at you at the airport.'

'He was probably staring at you. At *us*. Wondering how he could be unlucky enough to be partnered with my clone.'

'That bad, huh?'

'Yep.' Hannah threw her suitcase onto the bed and snapped it open. 'No time for a shower, I don't suppose?'

'Not really. Sorry. Put your togs on under your clothes and take a towel. You can swim while I do my patient visits.' Susie made for the door. 'I'd better throw a shirt over this top so I look more respectable to go to work. It's lucky we don't stand on ceremony much around this place.'

It was blissful, pulling off the denim and leaving Hannah's legs bare beneath the pretty, ruffled skirt that she chose. The lacy camisole top was perfectly decent seeing as she was wearing her bikini top instead of a bra. Hannah emerged from the room a minute later to find Susie looking thoughtful.

'I just can't believe that the guy Emily was telling me about is the same guy you've been describing. As far as Mike's concerned, he's a hero. Practically a saint.'

Hannah dampened the image she had of Ryan when he was about to ignore the captain's direction to stay safely seated during severe turbulence to go and help where he was needed. He certainly had the courage that provided hero material. But a saint? No saint could get away with emitting that kind of sexual energy.

'Mike's not a woman,' she said firmly. 'I doubt there's a saintly bone in that body.'

'You could be right.' Susie's forget-me-not blue eyes, the exact match of Hannah's, were still dreamy. 'He's got that "bad boy" sort of edge, hasn't he?'

'I wouldn't say it like it's a compliment.'

Susie closed the front door behind them. 'Shall we walk? It's only a few minutes if you don't mind being blown about.'

'Yes, let's blow the cobwebs away. I could do with stretching my legs after all the sitting in planes.'

With a bit of luck, the wind might blow the current topic of conversation away as well.

No such luck.

'You have to admit, it's attractive.'

'What is?'

'That "bad boy" stuff. The idea that some guy could give you the best sex you've ever had in your life because he's had enough practice to be bloody good at it.'

Hannah laughed, catching her skirt as it billowed up to reveal her long legs. A car tooted appreciatively as it shot past. Thank goodness she was wearing a respectable bikini bottom instead of a lacy number or a thong and that her summer tan hadn't begun to fade yet. Despite being blonde and blue-eyed, she and Susie both tanned easily without burning.

'I don't do one-night stands or even flings,'

Hannah reminded Susie. 'You know perfectly well the kind of trouble they lead to.'

'Yeah.' But Susie seemed to have finally got over her last heartbreak. 'But you always think you might just be the one who's going to make them want to change. And they're such *fun* at the time. To begin with, anyway.'

They walked in silence for a minute and Hannah looked down the grassy slope dotted with rocks and yellow flowers that led to the beach. A quite impressive surf from the murky sea was sending foamy scum to outline the distance up the beach the waves were reaching.

'You've never done it, have you?' Susie asked finally. 'Let your hair down and gone with sheer physical attraction? Slept with someone on a first date or fallen in love just because of the way some guy *looks* at you.'

'Never.' If she said it firmly enough she could convince herself as well, couldn't she? She couldn't admit, even to Susie, how often Ryan infiltrated her thoughts in the small hours of the night. It was lust she felt for the man. Nothing more.

Or should that be *less?*

'Sometimes I wish I were as strong as you,' Susie said wistfully.

'Someone had to be, in our family. The voice of reason, that's what I was. The devil's advocate.'

'You were always good at picking out what was wrong with the men Mum brought home.'

'Just a pity she never listened to me. She lost the house because she went ahead and married that slimeball, Richard the first.'

'Yeah. At least she's happy now. Or seems to be. Jim adores her.'

'And he's comfortably off and perfectly sensible. I'm sure Mum's learned to love fishing.'

'Hmm.'

Hannah couldn't blame Susie for sounding dubious. She made a mental note to ring her mother as soon as she got home.

'Come this way.' Susie pointed away from the signs directing people to the emergency and other departments of Crocodile Creek Base Hospital. 'We'll cut through the garden to the doctors' house and I can show you the pool and then shoot off and see those patients. Might be better if we leave the hospital tour until Sunday. Your flight doesn't leave till the afternoon, does it?'

'3 p.m.'

'Bags of time. I'll be able to introduce you properly to every hungover staff member we come across instead of confusing you with too many names.'

'I'll meet them at the wedding in any case.'

'You'll meet a few of them tonight. We're hoping to whisk Emily away after the rehearsal and take her out to dinner to give her a kind of hens' night. Which reminds me, I need to pop into the house and see who's going to be around. Gina might be there and Georgie should be back by now.'

'Is the dinner going to be at the Athina?'

'Heavens, no! Sophia already has the tables set up and about three thousand white bows tied to everything. She'll be making the family eat in the kitchens tonight, I expect—or they'll be roasting a lamb on a spit down on the beach. Such a shame about this weather.'

The lush tropical garden they were entering provided surprisingly good shelter from the wind thanks to the thick hibiscus hedges, and Hannah found she was too hot and sticky again.

Her head was starting to throb as well, probably due to dehydration.

'Any chance of a glass of water?'

'Sure. Come up to the house with me.'

Skirting a sundial in the centre of the garden, Hannah could hear the sound of laughter and splashing water. An irresistibly cool, swimming pool sort of sound. The pool was behind a fenced area, screened by bright-flowered shrubs that smelt gorgeous, but Hannah didn't get time for a proper look because Susie was already half way up a set of steps that led to the wide veranda of a huge old two-storey building. Following her, Hannah found herself in a large kitchen and gratefully drank a large glass of water while Susie dashed off to see who was at home.

'There's nobody here,' she announced on her return. 'Come on, I'll bet they're all in the pool as it's still lunchtime.'

The air of too much to get done in the available time was contagious and Hannah hurriedly rinsed her glass and left it upside down on the bench amongst plates that held the remains of what looked like some of Mrs Grubb's legendary chicken salad sandwiches. Susie was a woman on a mission as she sped out of the house and she was only momentarily distracted by the bumbling shape of a large, strangely spotty dog that bounded up the steps to greet her.

'Rudolf!' Susie put her arm out as though she intended to pat the dog, and Hannah had no idea what happened. A split second later, Susie was tumbling down the steps with a cry that was far from the delighted recognition of the dog and then—there she was—a crumpled heap at the bottom.

'*Susie!* Oh, my God! Are you all right?'

Hannah wasn't the only one to rush to her sister's rescue. More than one dripping figure emerged through the open gate in the swimming-pool fence.

Two men were there almost instantly. And one of them was Ryan.

'What's happened?'

'She fell down the steps. There was this dog.'

'Damn, who left the gate open?' Another dark-haired man with a towel wrapped around his waist appeared behind the others. 'CJ, you were supposed to be watching Rudolf.'

'I was being a *shark!*' A small wet boy wriggled

past the legs of the adults to stare, wide-eyed, at Susie. 'I had to be underwater,' he continued excitedly. 'With my fin on top—like this.' He stuck a hand behind his neck but no one was watching.

'It wasn't Rudolf's fault.' Susie was struggling into a sitting position. 'It's all right. I'm all right.'

'Are you sure?' A man with black curly hair and a gorgeous smile was squatting in front of Susie. 'You didn't hit your head, did you?'

'No. I don't know what happened, Mike. I just... Oh-h-h!'

'What's wrong?' Ryan moved closer. 'What's hurting?'

'My ankle,' Susie groaned. 'I think it's broken.'

'Just as well Luke's here, then,' Mike said, turning to another man who had approached the group. 'And they say you can't find an orthopaedic surgeon when you need one?'

'I *don't* need a surgeon,' Susie gulped. 'I hope.'

'I'll just be on standby,' Luke assured her. 'I am on babysitting duties after all.'

'*I'm* not a baby,' CJ stated. His hand crept into Luke's. 'You said I was your *buddy*.'

'You are, mate. You are...'

'Let *me* have a look.' Ryan's hands were on

Susie's ankle. He eased off her sandal before palpating it carefully. 'I can't feel anything broken.'

'Ouch!'

'Sorry. Sore in there, is it? Can you wiggle your toes?'

There was a small movement. 'Ouch,' Susie said again. She looked close to tears and Hannah crouched beside her, putting an arm around her shoulders. 'I don't believe this. How could I have done something this stupid?'

'Accidents happen,' Ryan said calmly. He laid his hand on top of Susie's foot. 'Can you stop me pushing your foot down?'

'No. Oh, that *really* hurts.'

'It's starting to swell already.' Hannah peered anxiously at Susie's ankle. She might not have been very impressed if this injury was in front of her in the emergency department, but this was no professional environment and this was her sister. And Ryan looked nothing like he did in the ED. Hannah's gaze swung back to her colleague for a moment. He was practically naked, for heaven's sake. Tanned and dripping and…gorgeous. And giving Susie that killer smile.

'I think it's just a bad sprain but we'll need an X-ray to be sure. At least you chose the right place. I believe there's an X-ray department not far away.'

'It's not funny,' Susie wailed. 'I've got to wear high heels tomorrow. Little white ones with a rose on the toe. My dress is nowhere long enough to cover an ankle the size of an elephant's. I need some ice. Fast.' Susie leaned down to poke at the side of her ankle. 'What if it's broken and I need a cast? Oh, Mike, I'm so sorry! This is a *disaster!*'

'Forget it,' the curly haired man told her. 'The only thing that matters right now is making sure you're all right. Let's get you over to A and E.'

'I'll take her,' Ryan offered. 'Isn't Emily expecting you back at the Athina?'

Mike glanced at his watch and groaned. 'Ten minutes ago. And I'm supposed to have all the latest printouts from the met bureau. The women are all petrified that Willie's going to turn back and ruin the wedding.'

'As if!' Luke was grinning. 'There's no way Sophia's going to let a bit of weather undermine a Poulos wedding.'

Hannah could feel an increasing level of

tension curling inside her. This was no time to be discussing the weather. Or a wedding. Susie needed attention. Her sister's face was crumpling ominously.

'*I'm* ruining the wedding,' she wailed forlornly. 'How could I have been so *stupid?*'

Hannah glared at Ryan. If he made even one crack about anything blonde, he would have to die!

Ryan's eyebrows shot up as he caught the force of the warning. Then he looked away from Hannah with a tiny, bemused shake of his head.

'Nothing else hurting?' he asked Susie. 'Like your neck?'

She shook her head.

'Right. Let's get this sorted, then.'

With an ease that took Hannah's breath away, Ryan took charge. He scooped Susie into his arms as though she weighed no more than the little boy, CJ. 'Emergency's that way, yes?'

'Yes,' Luke confirmed. 'Through the memorial garden.'

'Can I go, too?' CJ begged. ' I want to watch.'

'No,' Luke said. 'We told Mom we'd be waiting here when she got back.'

Mike was grinning broadly. 'You sure you want to go in like that, mate?'

'No time to waste.' Ryan was already moving in the direction Hannah had approached earlier. 'We need ice. And an X-ray.'

Hannah was only too pleased to trot behind Ryan. This was exactly the action that was required and there was no way she could have carried Susie herself.

'I'll bring your clothes over,' Mike called after them. 'I'll just call Emily and let her know what's happening.'

What was happening was a badly sprained ankle.

Despite ice and elevation and firm bandaging, Susie's ankle was continuing to swell impressively and was far too painful to put any weight on at all.

'Crutches.' An older and clearly senior nurse appeared in the cubicle Susie was occupying nearly an hour later. 'At least I won't need to give you a rundown on how to use them, Susie.'

'Thanks, Jill.' But Susie took one look at the sturdy, wooden, underarm crutches and then covered her face with her hands as though struggling not to burst into tears.

There was a moment's heavy silence. The cubicle was quite crowded what with Hannah standing by the head of Susie's bed, Ryan—now dressed, thankfully—and Mike leaning on the wall and Jill at the foot of the bed, holding the horrible accessories Susie was not going to be able to manage without.

Then the silence was broken.

'What are you saying?' came a loud, horrified, female voice. 'She can't *walk?* How can we have a bridesmaid who can't *walk?*'

'Oh, no!' Susie groaned. 'Sophia!'

'I was wondering how she'd take the news,' Mike said gloomily. 'Em didn't sound too thrilled either.'

A young woman with honey-blonde hair and rather serious grey-blue eyes rushed into the cubicle.

'Susie, are you all right? Is it broken?' She leaned over the bed to hug her friend. 'You poor thing!'

Hannah's eyes widened as the curtain was flicked back decisively. It wasn't just Mike's mother who had accompanied Emily. There were at least half a dozen women and they were all talking at once. Loudly. Anxiously.

'Susie! Darling!' The small, plump woman at the forefront of the small crowd sailed into the cubicle and stared at Hannah. 'What *have* you done to your hair?'

'I'm not Susie,' Hannah said weakly, as her sister emerged from Emily's hug. 'I'm her twin, Hannah.'

'Oh, my God!' The young, dark-haired woman beside Sophia was also staring. 'You *are* identical. Look at that, Ma! You wouldn't be able to tell them apart.'

An excited babble and an inward flow of women made Hannah back into the corner a little further. Alarmed, she looked for an escape route, only to catch the highly amused faces of both Mike and Ryan. There was nothing for it but to hold her breath and submit to the squash of people both wanting to pat and comfort Susie and to touch Hannah and see if she was actually real.

Jill looked as though she knew even her seniority would be no help in trying to evict this unruly mob from her emergency department and was taking the crutches out of the way for the moment, but the movement attracted Sophia's attention.

'What are those?'

'Susie's crutches.' Jill picked up speed as she backed away.

'She needs *crutches?*' Sophia crossed herself, an action that was instantly copied by all the other relatives. 'But we can't have crutches! The photographs!'

'It's all right, Ma.' The woman who had to be Mike's sister, Maria, was grinning. 'It doesn't matter if Susie can't walk.'

'It doesn't matter? Of course it matters!' Sophia's arms were waving wildly and Hannah pressed herself further into the corner. 'There are six dresses. We have to have six bridesmaids and Susie is Emily's best friend. She has to be in the photographs. In the ceremony.' A lacy handkerchief appeared from someone's hand and Sophia dabbed it to her eyes. 'But with crutches? Oh, no, no, no…' The sympathetic headshakes from all directions confirmed that this event was cataclysmic.

'Never mind Willie,' Mike murmured audibly to Ryan. 'This is going to be worse than any cyclone, believe me.'

'Ma, listen!' Sophia's shoulders were firmly grasped by Maria. 'We can use Hannah instead.'

'*What?*' The word was wrenched from Hannah and everybody was listening now. And staring. And then talking, all at once.

'No, her hair's all wrong.'

'She's the same size. She'll fit the dress.'

'Nothing that curling tongs couldn't fix.'

'No crutches!'

'Nobody will know the difference.'

'I'll know,' Emily said emphatically. 'And so will Susie.' She still had her arms protectively around her friend.

'Would it matter?' Susie spoke only to Emily. 'I'd rather it was Hannah than me in the photos, Em. I'd just spoil them.'

'No, you wouldn't.'

'Yes, I would. It would be the first thing anyone would notice when they looked at the pictures. Or when they're sitting in the church. Instead of saying, "Look at that gorgeous bride," they'd be saying, "Why is that girl on crutches? What's wrong with her?"'

The chorus of assent from the avid audience was unanimous. Emily looked appealingly at Mike but he just shrugged sympathetically and then grinned.

'Up to you, babe,' he said, 'but it does seem fortuitous that you chose a chief bridesmaid that's got a spare copy of herself available.'

Hannah looked at Ryan. If this crazy solution was going to make everybody happy then of course she would have to go along with it. But would Ryan?

Clearly, it *was* going to make everybody happy. Especially Susie.

'I'll still be there,' she was telling Emily. 'And Hannah's like part of me anyway.'

'Hannah? Are you OK with this?'

'Sure.' Hannah smiled warmly at Emily. 'I'd be honoured.'

'Hannah! Darling!' Sophia was reaching to squeeze Hannah's cheeks between her hands. 'Thank you! Thank you!'

Nobody asked Ryan if he was OK with the plan. Hannah caught his gaze and for a moment they just stared at each other. Another moment of connection. They were the two outsiders. Caught up in a circus over which they had no hope of exerting the slightest control.

It was a bit like dealing with the turbulence on that plane trip really. Had that been only this morning? Fate seemed determined to hurl them together. As closely as possible.

Ryan's expression probably mirrored her own. There was nothing they could do about it so they may as well just go with the flow.

There was something else mixed in with the resignation. Maybe it was due to the almost joyous atmosphere in the cubicle at having solved a potentially impossible hitch to the perfect wedding. Or maybe, for Hannah, it was due to something she didn't want to analyse.

It was more than satisfaction.

Curiously, it felt more like excitement.

CHAPTER FIVE

CLOUDS were rolling in towards the North Queensland coast by 5 p.m.

Stained-glass windows in the small, Greek Orthodox church in the main township of Crocodile Creek were rattled with increasing force by the sharp wind gusts.

'Did you hear that?' Emily tugged on Mike's arm. 'It's getting worse.'

'Last report was that Willie's heading further out to sea. Stop fretting, babe. Spit for luck instead.'

'I've given up spitting, I told you that.' The smile Emily shared with her fiancé spoke of a private joke and Hannah found herself smiling as well. Emily and Mike had the kind of bond she had only ever found with her sister. One where an unspoken language said so much and just a look or a touch could convey a lot more than words.

If she was ever going to get married herself, Hannah would want that kind of a bond with the man she was going to spend the rest of her life with. She had known it wouldn't be easy to find a man she could trust to that extent. No, that wasn't quite true. Trevor had been as reliable and trustworthy as it was possible to be—perhaps because he was so hard working and scientific and couldn't tolerate anything that required imagination or spontaneity.

The relationship had gone from one of comfort to one of predictability. And then boredom had set in. In the end, Hannah had been quietly suffocating. The opportunity that moving to Auckland to take up her first registrar position had afforded had been too good to miss. Much to poor Trevor's unhappy bewilderment, she had also moved on from their relationship.

She hadn't been in another relationship since. Hurting another nice, kind, trustworthy man was not on the agenda. Risking personal disaster by trying the kind of man who was fascinating was also a place Hannah had no intention of going. Of course Susie was right. That 'bad boy' edge was attractive. It would be all too easy to think like most women—that *they* would be the one to make the difference—but it never happened like that. Not in real life.

Emily tore her eyes away from Mike to smile apologetically at Hannah. 'I must sound like a real worry wart,' she said, 'but I've got a long veil. Can you imagine what it's going to be like in gale-force winds?'

'There are six of us.' Hannah glanced at the lively group of young women milling behind her that included Mike's sister, Maria. 'I'm sure we'll be able to keep your veil under control.'

Sophia put the finishing touches to yet another of the large, alternating peach and white bows she was tying to the ends of the pews and then clapped her hands.

'Another practice!' she ordered. 'Michael! What are you doing? Go back up to the front with the others. Ryan! You're supposed to be making my son behave.'

'That'll be the day,' Ryan muttered. 'Come on, mate. Let's get this over with and then we can hit the bright lights of Crocodile Creek for a stag party, yes?'

'That really *would* be the day,' Mike responded

with a grimace. 'There's a lamb on a spit turning as we speak and every member of the family has about six jobs to do later. I think you're down for potato-peeling duties. Or possibly painting the last of the damn chicken bones.'

'Chicken bones?'

'Quickly!' Sophia's tone suggested that there would be trouble if co-operation did not take place forthwith.

The two men shared a grin and then ambled up the red carpet of the aisle, and the rear view made Hannah realise how similar they were. Both tall and dark and handsome. They were wearing shorts and T-shirts at the moment but Hannah could well imagine what they'd look like tomorrow in their dark suits, crisp white shirts and bow ties. Just…irresistible.

Emily was watching the men as well and she sighed happily. 'I can't believe this is really going to happen,' she whispered. 'It's just too good to be true.'

Her eyes were shining and Hannah could feel the glow. What would it be like, she wondered, to be *that* happy? To be so sure you'd chosen the right person and that that kind of love had a good chance of lasting for ever? Mike looked like Ryan in more than an outward physical sense. They both had that laid-back, mischievous gleam that advertised the ability to get the most enjoyment possible out of life. And that did not generally include settling down with one woman and raising a family. Had Emily been the one to change Mike? Did being Greek make the difference? Or was she heading for unimaginable heartbreak?

No. Hannah didn't believe that for a moment. She had seen the way Mike and Emily had looked at each other. They had found the real thing, all right. Standing in this pretty church, about to rehearse the steps for a ceremony to join two lovers in matrimony, Hannah couldn't help a flash of envy. It was a bit like winning the lottery, wasn't it? Only it was a human lottery and you couldn't buy tickets. And even if you were lucky enough to find one, you might forget to read the small print and think you'd won, only to have the prize snatched away. It had happened to both her mother and to Susie, and Hannah knew why. Because 'the Richards' had had that hint of a 'bad boy' edge. They had been playboys. Fun-seekers. Like Ryan.

The pageboys and flower girls were being rounded up from their game of chase between the empty pews. They were holding plastic beach buckets as a prop to represent the baskets of petals they would hold tomorrow. Sophia herded them into place and repeated instructions they had apparently misheard on the first rehearsal.

'Gently!' she insisted. 'You are throwing rose petals, CJ, not sticks for Rudolf!'

Maria was examining her nails. 'They're full of silver paint,' she complained. 'I never want to see another chicken bone in my life.'

'What's with the chicken bones?' Hannah queried. 'I heard Mike saying something about them as well.'

'Wishbones.' Emily was moving to take her place in the foyer. 'Painted silver. Sophia's planning to attach them to the little bags of almonds the guests will be given. Not that anyone's found time to put the almonds in the bags yet, let alone attach the wishbones.'

'They're for fertility,' Maria added. 'The almonds, that is. And boy, do I wish they hadn't been scattered around at my wedding. Watch out for the ones in your bed, Em. I'd sweep them out if I were you or you might end up like me, with four little monsters under five.' She was peering anxiously past Hannah to see if her small children were doing what they were supposed to on reaching the end of the petal-throwing procession.

'Uncle Mike!' one of them shrieked. 'Did you see me pretending to throw petals?'

Mike swept the small girl into his arms and kissed her. Ryan held out his hands and got high-fives from two small boys—a gesture that was clearly well practised. Then he pulled them in, one on each side of his body, for a one-armed hug.

'Good job, guys,' Hannah heard him say.

When did Ryan get to spend enough time with young children to be that at ease with them? Did he have a big family with lots of nieces and nephews? Maybe he'd been married already and had his own children. The notion was quite feasible. It would explain his frequent trips back to Sydney. Not that it mattered to Hannah. She was just aware of how little she knew about her colleague. Aware of a curiosity she had no intention of satisfying.

'I hope the aisle's going to be wide enough.' Emily had come back to her cluster of bridesmaids. 'My dress is *huge*. A giant meringue. Do you think there'll be room for a wheelchair beside me?'

'A wheelchair?' Hannah was glad she'd paid attention to Susie's emails. 'Is Charles Wetherby giving you away?'

'Yes. He's the closest thing to a father figure I've got.'

Reading between the lines of those emails, Hannah had the impression that Charles was a father figure to more than just Emily. With an ability to know more about what was happening within the walls of the hospital he directed than his staff were always comfortable with. A man with a quiet strength and wisdom that provided the cement for a remarkable small community of professional medics. A community that her sister was very much a part of now.

'I'm sure there'll be room,' she said confidently.

'Susie!' Sophia was sounding flustered. She was waving frantically from the altar end of the aisle. 'Pay attention, darling!'

'It's Hannah, Ma, not Susie,' Maria shouted.

'I knew that. You know what I mean. Come on, girls. In your pairs.'

Hannah and Maria were first. They walked along the red carpet beneath the elaborate chandelier, the gilt frame of which had miniature copies of the paintings of various saints that decorated the walls of this church between the stained-glass windows. The tiny crystals tinkled musically overhead as another gust of wind managed to shake the solid brick building.

Maria glanced up at the chandelier and muttered something under her breath that could have been either a curse or a prayer. Maybe a bit of both, Hannah decided, as Mike's sister flashed a grin at her.

'It's going to be a wild wedding at this rate!'

Hannah nodded agreement but found herself swallowing a little nervously. Even if Willie was out to sea and moving in a safe direction, this was still as close to a tropical cyclone as she felt comfortable with.

The first rehearsal made it easy to remember what to do this time. Hannah and Maria climbed to the top of the three steps and then waited until the other pairs of bridesmaids were on the lower steps before they all turned gracefully in unison to watch the bride's entrance.

Hannah felt a complete fraud. If only Emily and Susie weren't so set on her standing in. She couldn't even follow someone else's lead. She was the chief bridesmaid. It was up to her to make sure all the others did the right thing at the right time. There was a point when she would actually be a closer part of this ceremony, too. When the bride and groom were wearing the matching orange-blossom wreaths on their heads that were joined by satin ribbons, they would take their first steps as man and wife with a tour three times around the altar. It would be Hannah's job to hold up the train of Emily's dress and keep her veil in order. As best man, Ryan would be right beside her, holding up the ribbons joining the wreaths.

He would be wearing his tuxedo and Hannah would be so dressed up and groomed she wouldn't even feel like herself. She would have to be Ryan's partner in this ceremony and probably at the reception. She might even have to dance with him, and she was going to feel so uncomfortable she would be hating every minute of it.

And you'll look miserable, a small voice at the back of her mind warned. You'll make Susie miserable and probably Emily and definitely Ryan, and they'll all wish you'd never been invited to this wedding. Hannah noticed the nudge that Mike gave his best man by bumping shoulders. There was a whispered comment and then a frankly admiring stare from both men as the girls behind Hannah proudly arranged themselves on the steps. The men grinned approvingly. The girls giggled. They were all enjoying every moment of this circus.

And why not? It was going to be a huge party. The wild weather would probably only enhance the enjoyment of those safely tucked away inside. It was play time, not work time. Why couldn't she just relax and have fun, like they were?

Everybody thought she was boring. Too focussed on her career. Too ready to trouble-shoot problems before they even occurred. It should, and probably did, make her a very good doctor, but too many people had criticised that ability in the last few days. Jennifer thought she had no life of her own outside work. Ryan thought she was dull. Even her own sister had

commented on her lack of spontaneity or will-
ingness to reap the rewards of taking a personal
risk.

Hannah had never allowed sheer physical attraction to be the deciding factor when it came
to men. Or slept with someone on a first date.
Not that she intended to jump Ryan's bones, of
course. Or fall in love with him because of a
look, or, in his case, more likely due to the kind
of smile she'd experienced in the plane that
morning. The kind her junior bridesmaids were
enjoying right now.

She could, however, throw caution to the
winds for once, couldn't she? Given the current
weather conditions in Crocodile Creek, it would
be highly likely to be blown a very long way
away, but would that be so terrible?

For the next twenty-four hours or so, she was
going to have to pretend to be Susie. Someone
with a rather different perspective on life and
taking risks. This could be the perfect opportunity to step outside her own comfort zone. To
really let her guard down and simply enjoy the
moment, without trying to see down the track to
locate potential hazards.

What did she have to lose? On Sunday she would get on a plane again to go home. Back to being herself. Back to working hard enough to ensure the success she craved. Hopefully, back to a new position as an emergency department consultant. And how much time would she get to have fun after that? This weekend could be seen as a kind of hens' party really. A final fling before Hannah became wedded to a new and intense phase of her career.

And it wouldn't hurt to show Ryan Fisher that she *did* know how to enjoy herself. That she wasn't all work and no play and as dull as ditchwater.

Yes!

Hannah hunched her shoulders and then let them drop to release any unconscious tension.

And then she smiled at Ryan. Really smiled. Here we are, then, her smile said. Let's have fun!

Good grief!

What had he done to deserve a smile like that? One that actually touched Hannah's eyes instead of just being a polite curve of her lips.

Ryan had to fight the urge to glance over his

shoulder to see whether the real recipient of the smile was standing nearby.

Hell, she was gorgeous. It was going to be more than rather difficult to stick to his resolution if she was going to do things like smile at him like that. Almost as bad as discovering it had been Hannah and not Susie wearing that frilly skirt. The one that the wind had whipped up to reveal a pair of extremely enticing legs as he and Mike had driven up to the hospital earlier that afternoon. He'd never be able to see her wearing scrubs trousers in the ED again without knowing what lay beneath the shapeless fabric.

Mind you, that hadn't been half as disconcerting as what had happened later. Ryan had been entertaining hopes of finding Susie's company perfectly enjoyable. Of maybe being able to learn why his attractive colleague was so uptight and had taken such an instant dislike to him.

To have Susie incapacitated and Hannah stepping in to fill the breach had been a cruel twist of fate. Not that he'd allowed his disappointment to show, of course. Not when Emily had looked so happy. When Emily looked that happy, Mike was happy. And if his best buddy was happy, Ryan certainly wasn't going to do anything to tarnish the glow.

He'd go through with this and he'd look as if he was enjoying every moment of it. It would be hard *not* to enjoy it, in fact, and if he could only make sure his resolution regarding Hannah Jackson didn't go out the window, he could be sure he wouldn't spoil that enjoyment by getting some kind of personal putdown.

But it would help—a lot—if she didn't smile at him like that. As though she had put aside her preconceived and unflattering opinions. Opened a window in that wall of indifference to him and was seeing him—*really* seeing him— for the first time.

She did look a bit taken aback when he offered to take her home after the rehearsal but she rallied.

'Sure. I guess it's on your way, seeing as you're staying in the doctors' house. I might even go as far as the hospital and check on Susie.'

'It's good that she decided she would stay in overnight and get that intensive RICE treatment. It should help a lot.'

'Mmm.' Hannah's tone suggested that nothing

would help enough unless, by some miracle, Susie awoke after a night of compression bandages and ice and elevation to find her foot small enough to wear her shoe and the ability to stand and walk unaided, which was highly unlikely. 'I need to stop at her house and collect a few things she might need, if you're not in too much of a hurry.'

'Not at all.' Ryan lowered his voice. 'With a bit of luck, I'll arrive at the Athina *after* all the potatoes are peeled.'

Hannah made no response to that and Ryan kicked himself mentally. What was he trying to do here? Prove how shallow and lazy he was?

'Tell Susie I'll be up to see her later,' Emily said as they left the church. 'If she can't come to the hens' party, we'll just have to take the party to her.'

'I think Jill might have something to say about that,' Mike warned. 'She's not big on parties happening in her wards.'

'Yeah.' Emily nodded sadly. 'She'd say that I should know the R in RICE stands for rest. Tell Susie I'll come and get her later in the morning, then, so she can come and supervise. Kylie can still do her hair and make-up.'

To Ryan's disappointment, Hannah was ready for the wind when they stepped outside. She had wrapped her skirt firmly around those long brown legs and was holding it in place. On the positive side, the action affected her balance and a good gust sent her sideways a few moments later to bump into Ryan. She could have fallen right over, in fact, if he hadn't caught her arms.

Bare arms.

Soft skin.

Enough momentum in the movement for Ryan to feel the press of her breasts against his hands. It wasn't the first time he had touched her skin but the tension of that incident in the plane hadn't really afforded an opportunity to analyse the effect. It was, quite simply, electrifying. Or was that because this contact had come about so unexpectedly?

No. He'd known, all along, that there would be something very different about touching this woman.

Something very special.

He didn't want to let go. The urge to pull her even closer and kiss her senseless was as powerful as what felt like hurricane-force winds funnelling through the church car park, whipping their hair and buffeting their bodies.

Simply irresistible.

Oh…*God!*

The strength of the grip Ryan had on her arms was sending shock waves through Hannah, not to mention the delicious tingle of what had to be that latent lust kicking in.

And he looked…as though he wanted to *kiss* her!

Even more shocking was the realisation that she *wanted* him to.

Letting her hair down and being prepared to enjoy this weekend was one thing. Making out with Ryan Fisher in a church car park was quite another. And quite unacceptable.

Hannah wrenched herself free. 'You've got Mike's car?'

'Yes. That Jeep over there.'

The vehicle was vaguely familiar. Hadn't that been the one that had hooted when her skirt had blown up around her neck on that walk around the cove? Had it been Ryan getting a close-up view of her legs?

The tingle became a shaft of something much stronger that was centred deep in Hannah's abdomen but sent spirals all the way to the tips of her fingers and toes. Battling with the door of the Jeep so it didn't catch in the wind and fly outwards was a welcome diversion. Why was she feeling like this? Had she somehow flicked a mental switch back there in the church that could lead her rather too far into temptation?

How inappropriate.

But intriguing.

Ryan wouldn't think twice about following his inclinations, would he? Sleeping with someone on a first date or having a little weekend fling? Hannah couldn't help casting a speculative glance at her companion as he started the Jeep and they moved off. His hands gripped the steering-wheel with enough strength to keep the vehicle straight despite the strong winds but they didn't look tense. Strength and a capacity to be gentle. What had Susie said about bad boys and getting the best sex you ever had?

Maybe her thoughts were too powerful. Something made Ryan turn his head. He held her gaze for only a heartbeat and then gave her one of those smiles.

Oh…help! Hannah spent the next few minutes until they were driving over that rickety bridge wondering if Ryan was discreet. Whether what happened on camp would stay on camp. Seeing as she'd never actually heard any firsthand gossip about his previous conquests, it seemed likely that the answer was yes. The added bonus of dealing with that distracting attraction as well as proving she could be fun might well mean that her working relationship with Ryan could be vastly improved. Even when she got the consultancy position and, effectively, became his boss.

It was quite difficult to rein in her thoughts and focus on her immediate intentions.

'I might change my clothes before I go and visit Susie.' Thinking out loud was partly to ensure Ryan didn't know what she'd really been thinking about. 'I've still got my bikini on under this and it's not as if I'm going to get a chance to swim.'

'That's a shame. The pool's great. Very refreshing.'

'It has been a long day, hasn't it?' Hannah

agreed. 'Feels like for ever since we left Auckland.' A different time. A different place. Different rules were definitely allowable.

'You could have a swim after you've been visiting.'

'I'd still need a change of clothes and, besides, it gets dark early here, doesn't it?'

'About eight, I think. But there are lights around the pool. People often swim at night over summer from what Mike was telling me.'

'Tempting. I might just do that. This heat is really getting to me.' It wasn't the first time that day that Hannah had lifted the weight of hair off her neck to try and cool down a fraction. 'I don't think I've ever felt this hot in my life.'

'Mmm. You look pretty hot.' Ryan's grin suggested that he was commenting on her sexual appeal rather than her body temperature but, for once, Hannah wasn't put off. Was that because the flirtatious comment was acceptable under the new rules that seemed to be forming?

She laughed. 'You're hopeless, Ryan.' Then she pointed ahead. 'Stop here—that's Susie's cottage.'

Ryan followed her as far as the veranda. When Hannah emerged a few minutes later, wearing light cargo pants and a shirt over her bikini and with a towel and underwear and things for Susie in a carry bag, he was lounging against one of the posts framing the steps. Strands of bougainvillea snapped in the wind and a shower of dark red petals had left blooms caught in the dark waves of his hair.

'Why am I hopeless?'

Had he been stewing over the casual reprimand the whole time he had been waiting for her?

'Because you're an incorrigible flirt,' Hannah informed him. 'You can't talk to women without…' She had to leave the sentence unfinished. 'Without making them feel like you're attracted to them' had been the words on the tip of her tongue but what would happen if he responded by saying he *was* attracted to her? In theory, letting her hair down was great, but this was actually quite scary. What if he said she had nothing to worry about because there was no way he could be attracted to her? Hannah's mouth felt oddly dry.

'Most women appreciate a compliment,' Ryan was saying. 'I try to be nice. To establish a good rapport with the people I work with.'

'Hmm.' Hannah didn't have to try and make the sound less than understanding. Professional rapport had boundaries that Ryan clearly took no notice of.

He hadn't moved from the support of the post. To get to the car, Hannah had to go down the steps, which meant moving closer to the stationary figure.

'I work with you, Dr Jackson.'

'You do, Dr Fisher.' Hannah gripped the handles of her carry bag more firmly and made the move to the top of the steps.

'I'd like *us* to establish a good rapport. I don't think we've really got one yet, have we?'

'No.' She was close to Ryan now. She could almost have reached out and plucked petals from his hair.

'Why is that, Hannah?'

'I...ah...' It had been a mistake to make eye contact at this proximity. Words totally failed Hannah.

'Maybe we could try again,' Ryan suggested softly. 'We're in a new place that has nothing to do with work. We could make this weekend a new start.'

'Ah…' Something had already started. Hannah watched the way Ryan's gaze slid from her eyes to her mouth. The way his head was tilting slightly. She had to close her eyes as a wave of desire threatened to make her knees wobble and send her down the steps in an undignified stagger.

Had she mirrored that tilt of his face? Leaned closer to Ryan? Or had he just closed the gap of his own accord so that he could kiss her?

Not that it mattered. The instant his lips touched hers, *nothing* else mattered.

Yes, it was the start of something new, for sure. Something Hannah had never experienced. The first brush of paint on a totally new canvas.

Soft lips. A gentle pressure. Long enough to be intensely arousing but not nearly long enough. Hannah wanted more.

A *lot* more.

She wanted to taste this man. To touch him. To have him touch her. To fill in more of that canvas because she had no idea what colours and textures it would encompass or what the finished picture might be like. What that brief kiss *had* told her, however, was that the picture would be bigger and more exciting than any she'd ever seen.

It was Ryan who bent to pick up the carry bag, which had slipped, unnoticed, from Hannah's fingers.

'This way, Dr Jackson,' he murmured. 'Your chariot awaits.'

Hannah didn't want to move. Unless it was to go back into the cottage and take Ryan with her. It was disappointing that he hadn't suggested it himself. Surely he would normally follow through on a kiss like that?

Perhaps he intended to. He smiled at Hannah.

'Maybe,' he said lazily, 'we can do something else about establishing that rapport later.'

'Rapport, huh? That's a new word for it.' Susie lay on her hospital bed with her leg elevated on pillows, bandaged and packed in ice. 'So what was it like, then?'

'The kiss?' Hannah chewed the inside of her cheek. 'Not bad, I guess.'

Susie pulled a pillow from behind her back to throw at her sister.

'OK, it was great. Best kiss I've ever had. Satisfied?'

'No. Are you?'

Hannah smiled wryly. 'No.'

'So what are you going to do about it?'

'What can I do? OK, he might have been tempted to kiss me for some reason but I can't see it going any further. He doesn't even like me. I don't like him. I'm just...attracted to him physically.'

'Maybe he's pretending not to like you because he's really attracted to you and you haven't given him any encouragement.'

'I kissed him! What more encouragement could he need?'

'Maybe he likes to take things slowly.'

'Ha!'

'Yeah.' Susie grinned. 'He doesn't look the type to take things slowly. Never mind, you've got the whole weekend in a tropical paradise. Something's bound to happen.'

'Forty-eight hours isn't that long.'

'But weddings are very romantic. And it's not as if you won't be seeing each other after you go home.'

'We won't be "seeing" each other when we go home. This is purely physical, Susie. An opportunity to get it out of my system. I mean, what if I'm sitting in a rest home when I'm ninety-five and I regret never trying a one-night stand? Doubt that I'd have the opportunity then.'

'So Ryan's not a long-term prospect, then?'

'Are you kidding? Would you take up with Richard the second with the benefit of hindsight?'

'No... Yes... Maybe...' Susie sighed. 'But Ryan might be different. He might not take off as soon as he spots greener pastures.'

'*Ha!*' Hannah put even more feeling into the dismissive response this time.

'Will you be seeing him again tonight?'

'No. I'm going to finish watching this movie with you, go and have a quick dip in the pool and then go home to sleep. I'm stuffed.'

'Why don't you skip the movie and see if you can find him over at the doctors' house? I've got some stuff about Emily I was going to tell him so he could put it in his best man's speech.'

Hannah groaned. 'He's probably got it written already. One long string of blonde jokes.'

'It's a good excuse to talk to him.'

'He'll be at the Athina. Peeling potatoes or something.'

'He might be back by now. He got up as early as you did so he's probably equally stuffed.'

'I could go and have a swim.'

'What's the weather like out there now?'

'Horribly windy but still hot. It's not raining.'

'The pool's nice and sheltered. You probably won't be the only one there. Lots of people like to cool off before they go to bed. You sleep a lot better that way.'

Hannah wasn't the only one in the pool.

Ryan was there.

'I've done my potato-peeling bit,' he told Hannah. He was watching her shed her outer clothing. 'I really needed to cool off.'

Hannah slid into the water with a sigh of pleasure. The pool area was sheltered but it was still windy enough to make the water slightly choppy and the wind on wet skin pulled the heat out quickly enough to raise goose-bumps when Hannah stood up at the shallower end of the pool. She ducked down and swam breaststroke into deeper water. 'This is gorgeous.'

'Isn't it?' Ryan was swimming towards her. Only his head was showing but, thanks to Susie's accident, Hannah was only too well aware of what the rest of Ryan looked like. She took a determined breath.

'Susie's been telling me things about Emily that might be useful for your best man's speech. Or have you finished writing it?'

Ryan grinned. 'No. Haven't started. Thought I might just wing it.'

'Well, there's a funny story about her spitting on Mike's helicopter.'

'Why did she do that?'

Hannah trod water, edging further away from Ryan. 'She was terrified of flying in helicopters and there's this Greek thing of spitting for luck. Only when the Greeks do it, it's kind of a token spit.' Hannah turned and swam a few strokes before shaking wet strands of hair from her eyes and taking another breath. 'When Emily did it, Mike had to clean the helicopter and there's a long-standing joke between them now about the paintwork getting corroded.' Hannah trod water again and turned. She should be a safe distance away from Ryan now.

She wasn't. He had kept pace with her.

'Interesting,' he said. 'I did know that Em

hated helicopters. The night Mike proposed to her, they'd been sent on a mission that got cancelled and he landed them on a secluded beach. She thought they were crashing so she was really angry but Mike said that emergency measures had been necessary because he really needed to talk to her.'

'It all worked out, then.'

'Mmm. They have a very good rapport.' Ryan twisted his body in the water so that he was floating on his back. 'How's our rapport coming along, Dr Jackson?'

'Pretty good, I think.' Was it a feeling of insecurity that made it a relief to find her feet could touch the bottom of the pool here?

'Could be better, though, couldn't it?' With a fishlike movement, Ryan turned again, moving sideways at the same time so that he was within touching distance of Hannah. He caught her shoulders and Hannah seemed to simply float into his arms.

Not that she tried to swim away. She could have. Her feet were secure on the tiles at the bottom of the pool as she stood up and it would have been possible to get enough momentum to escape.

But she had no intention of escaping. This was it. She just had to get over the fear of doing something so out of character. Falling into what looked like a matching desire in Ryan's dark eyes, it became possible to step over that boundary.

'Yes,' she managed to whisper.

And then he was kissing her again and it was totally different to that kiss on the veranda. This one had a licence to continue. This one rapidly deepened so that Hannah had to wind her arms around Ryan's neck to keep her head above water. She could feel his hands on her bare skin, along with ripples from the disturbed water that seemed to magnify the sensation. His fingers trailed from her neck down her back, held her waist and then stroked their way up to cup her breasts.

At the same time, his lips and tongue were doing things that were arousing Hannah more than she would have believed possible. His face and lips were cool, thanks to the relentless wind, but the inside of his mouth was far from cool. It was hot enough to fuel an already burning desire. Hannah kissed him back, sucked headlong into that desire until she totally forgot herself. When he held her closer, Hannah found herself winding her legs around Ryan so that she couldn't float away.

Ryan groaned. 'God,' he murmured, pulling her hips even closer with an urgent strength to his grip. 'I want you, Hannah. You know that, don't you?'

Hannah tried to swallow, but couldn't. 'I want you, too.'

'Not here. Somewhere dry.'

Hannah had all the incentive she needed to throw caution to the winds for at least one night of her life. She even managed to sound as though she was quite used to being carried away by physical passion.

'Your place or mine?' she asked with a smile.

'Mine's closer. Just up those steps. It's Mike's old room. You can get in through a door on the veranda so nobody will see us.' Ryan bent to kiss her again and then he took her hand in his to lead her from the pool. 'You sure about this, Hannah?'

'What's not to be sure of? As you said, it's important to establish a good rapport with the people you work with.' She tightened her fingers around his, shivering as she climbed the steps of the pool and the wind caught at more of her exposed skin. Or was it the thought of where she was going and what she knew they would do that caused that shiver? Not that she had any intention of backing out. No way.

'Lead on, Dr Fisher.'

CHAPTER SIX

IT WAS the curious howling sound that woke Ryan.

The first fingers of light were stretching under the roof of the wide veranda to enter his room and he could just make out the smooth hump of the feminine shoulder beside him.

Without thinking, Ryan touched the skin with his lips. A butterfly kiss that was as gentle as the way he traced the delicious curve of Hannah's hip with his hand, loving that dip to her waist that was accentuated by her lying on her side.

Loving everything about this woman. This new version of Hannah Jackson.

Her intensity. Softness. Suppleness. The way she accepted everything he had to offer and had responded in kind.

Thank God he hadn't stuck to that resolution to stay well away from her.

If he had, he would have missed out discovering just how good it was possible for sex to get. His experience last night had been the best he'd ever had in his life.

And Ryan knew what had made the difference. It was knowing he'd been right the moment he'd first laid eyes on Hannah. That there was a reason why the attraction had been so powerful. It was just possible he had found what he desperately needed in his life.

More of an anchor than a permanent job represented. The haven of a relationship that could be trusted. Could grow into something strong enough to last a lifetime. Could become a whole family even.

Something *good*. Love that wasn't darkened by the grim side of life. He was so tired of being strong for the people he loved. Not that he'd ever stop, but he badly needed something that would let the sunshine back into his own soul.

Someone he could be totally honest with. Someone that he could actually allow to see that things ripped him apart sometimes. He was fed up with hiding. Being flippant because he couldn't afford to share how he really felt.

Making other people laugh because he'd discovered that was the best way to escape his own fear or misery.

Not that he'd ever made Hannah really laugh and, in a way, that was scary. Could she see through him? Despise him for being less than honest with himself and others? Had she been hurt in the past by a man who hadn't been able to connect on an emotional level and was that why that prickly barrier had been between them since that first meeting? If so, he could understand. Forgive and forget any of the putdowns.

Ryan pressed another soft kiss to Hannah's shoulder. Then he lifted her hair to kiss the side of her neck. She'd dropped that barrier last night, hadn't she?

One night.

A perfect night.

Ryan let his breath out in a contented sigh. Never mind that dawn was breaking. Last night had been just the beginning. The connection had been established and it could be the foundation for something that was going to last for ever.

Right now, Ryan had no doubt that it was

entirely possible he could spend the rest of his life loving Hannah—in bed and out of it.

The dream took on colours that were so beautiful they took Hannah's breath away. She could actually *feel* them and the building excitement was something she remembered from childhood, waking up to a longed-for day that was going to bring something very special.

She was flying in her dream. Soaring over some incredible tropical landscape towards the place she most wanted to be. But she wasn't going to reach her destination because the edges of reality were pushing the dream away. The sense of loss was only momentary, however, because the reality was the touch of Ryan's lips. They were on the side of her neck, delivering a kiss so gentle it made her want to cry. Instinctively, she turned towards him, seeking the comfort of being held, only to find his lips tracing a line from her neck all the way to her breast. Stopping when they reached the apex and the cool flick of his tongue on her nipple took Hannah's breath away for real.

There was still a dreamlike quality to this, though, and Hannah kept her eyes closed even as her hands moved to find and touch Ryan where she now knew he most liked to be touched. The whole night had been a dream—the stuff of erotic fantasy—so why not keep it going just a little longer?

Thank God she had given in to that urge to experience something new. To find out if Susie was right and she'd discover the best sex of her life. Even in her wildest dreams until now, she hadn't had any idea what it could be like. Hannah could understand perfectly what had drawn her mother and her sister and probably countless other women into relationships that could only end in heartbreak.

Not that she was going to allow this to go that far. This was just a perfect ending to a perfect night. A one-night stand that Hannah could treasure the memory of for the rest of her life.

With a small sound of absolute pleasure, she slid her arms completely around Ryan to draw him closer.

It was raining when they woke again. Rain driven sideways by a wind that hadn't abated at all during the night. If anything, it was worse.

'What's the time?'

Ryan reached to collect the wristwatch he'd dropped by the side of the bed. 'Nearly nine.'

'Oh, my God, I can't believe we've slept in!' Hannah slid out from the tangled sheets, covering her bare breasts with her hands while she looked for her clothes. 'I've got to get back to Susie's place and get sorted. We're supposed to be at Kylie's salon by nine-thirty. It's probably chaos out there by now.'

'It would be chaos whatever time it is.' Ryan put his arms behind his head, clearly intending to watch Hannah getting dressed. 'Don't worry about it.'

'Where's my phone?' Hannah felt more in control now that she had her underwear on. 'Susie's probably been trying to text me. I put it on silent mode at the rehearsal yesterday and I completely forgot to reset it.'

'You got distracted,' Ryan said with satisfaction. 'The wedding's not till 4 p.m. Don't stress.'

Hannah pulled on crumpled cargo pants. Impossible not to feel stressed with the sound of rapid footsteps on the wooden boards of the veranda behind the thin curtain and then the excited bark of a dog.

'I need to get out of here without anyone seeing me.'

'Why?'

'It would be embarrassing if everyone knew I'd spent the night here.'

'Why?' Ryan repeated. 'It's nothing to be ashamed of. We're both single, consenting adults, aren't we?'

'Yes…' But there was an element of shame as far as Hannah was concerned. She'd never done anything like this in her life. This kind of selfish physical indulgence might be normal for Ryan and the women he chose, but it couldn't be more out of character for her. She'd always made sure she was ready to commit to an exclusive relationship before going to bed with someone.

'And it was fun, yes?' Ryan wriggled his eyebrows suggestively. 'I certainly enjoyed it.'

'Mmm.' Hannah tore her eyes away from the sight of Ryan getting out of bed. He obviously felt no need to cover himself. This was a man who was quite comfortable in his own skin. An enviable confidence that Hannah could only aspire to. She did her best. 'Me, too,' she added with a smile.

Ryan covered the floor space between them with an easy couple of strides. He drew Hannah into his arms and kissed her. 'I *really* enjoyed it,' he murmured. 'You're amazing.'

'Mmm.' The sound was a little strangled this time. Hannah wasn't so sure about daylight kisses. Sexual fantasy needed the cover of dark. She drew away. 'Could you keep an eye out and tell me when the coast is clear on the veranda? I can go down the other end, away from the kitchen, can't I?'

'Yeah.' Ryan turned away and picked up his shorts. 'I'll come with you.'

'No need. It'll only take me a few minutes to walk and I could do with the fresh air.'

'It'll be fresh all right. Might feel quite cold after yesterday with this rain. Did you bring a jacket?'

'No.'

'Then why don't you let me drive you home? I've got to take Mike's Jeep back up to the Athina, anyway. I'd better check in and see what my best-man duties involve. I suspect I'll have to stick with Mike for the rest of the day.'

And Hannah would need to be with Emily. She probably wouldn't see Ryan again till later that afternoon. No more daylight kisses to contend with. The odd sensation in her stomach had to be relief, rather than disappointment, surely?

'A ride would be good,' she said. 'That way I can get sorted faster.'

The veranda was deserted and no one interrupted their journey through the garden to the car park. As they scrambled from the end of the veranda, Ryan took hold of Hannah's hand and it felt so natural it would have been rude to pull hers away. As they left the gardens behind them, Hannah glanced at the hospital buildings but there had been no message from Susie yet and she would be back here in no time. Would she tell her sister about last night?

Maybe not. Not yet, anyway. The experience was still too fresh. Private and…precious?

Would Ryan say anything?

Maybe not. The way his hand still held hers was comforting. As though he shared a reluctance to break the illusion of a bond they'd created last night. Hannah was even more confident he could be discreet when he dropped her hand at the sight of someone running towards them.

Wet curls of black hair were plastered around Mike's face. 'I was just coming to find you, mate. Hi, Hannah.'

'What's up?' Ryan wasn't smiling. Neither was Mike.

'There's been an accident up at Wygera. Harry called me to see if I can do a first response with the Jeep. I've got a good paramedic kit in the back.' Mike was still moving and both Ryan and Hannah followed. 'I was on the way to the house to find a doc to come with me, but you'll do just fine.'

'Do you want me to come as well?' Hannah queried.

'Please.' Mike caught the keys Ryan threw and unlocked the doors of the Jeep. 'Sounds like there are at least three casualties. All teenagers.' He opened the back of the vehicle and pulled out a light, which he stuck to his roof. A cord snaked in through his window and he plugged the end into the cigarette lighter. A bright orange light started flashing as he turned on the engine.

'Where's Wygera?' Ryan pulled his safety belt on as Hannah climbed into the backseat.

'It's an aboriginal settlement about fifty miles from here. We'd normally get the chopper out for something like this but there's no way anyone's going to be flying today.' Gears crunched and the Jeep jerked backwards as Mike turned with speed and they took off. Hannah clicked her safety belt into its catch.

'What's happened?' she queried. 'And don't you have an ambulance available?'

'They're all busy on other calls right now and it'll take time to get a vehicle on the road. There's been trouble with the bloody bulls, by the sound of it—thanks to this weather.'

They were on the main road now, and Hannah could feel how difficult it was going to be, driving fast in the kind of wind gusts they were being subjected to. The windscreen wipers were on high speed but the rain appeared to be easing a little. Hannah shivered. She was damp and still hadn't had the opportunity to get any warmer clothing. Wrapping her arms around herself for warmth, she listened as Mike continued filling them in.

'There's a guy up at Wygera by the name of Rob Wingererra. They've acquired a few rodeo bulls. Long story, but they're a project for the teenagers up there. Huge animals with wicked horns. Apparently the wind caused some damage last night and brought a fence down and damaged a shed. The kids went out to try and get the bulls rounded up and into shelter and they got out of hand. Some kid's been cut by corrugated iron, one's been gored by a bull and another sounds like he might have a crush injury of some kind after getting caught between a bull and a gate.'

'How long will it take us to get there?'

'It's an hour's drive on a good day but I'm hoping to get there sooner than that. Hang on tight back there, Hannah, but don't worry. I know this road like the back of my hand. We'll just need to watch out for slips or rubbish on the road.'

He certainly knew the road. Having gone over the bridge and through the township, Mike headed towards the foothills of the mountains that divided the coastal plain from the cattle country Hannah knew was further inland. At the speed they were going, they would arrive there as fast as any ambulance was capable of. As they rounded one corner, Ryan threw a glance over his shoulder.

'You OK, Hannah?'

The tone was caring. How long had it been since a man had been this concerned for her well-being? It was dangerous to allow it to matter.

'I'm fine,' she said hurriedly.

'No, you're not—you're freezing!' Ryan twisted his body beneath the safety belt, pulling off the lightweight jacket he was wearing. 'Here. Put this on. '

'Thanks.' Hannah slid her arms into sleeves that were still warm from Ryan's skin. 'Are you sure you don't need it?'

But Ryan wasn't listening. 'What information have you been given about these kids so far?'

'There's a health worker at the settlement, Millie, who's very good. Rob called her after he found the kids and they've got them inside at his place. She's controlled the bleeding on the boy that got cut but it sounds like he might have lost quite a bit of blood. The one who got poked by a horn isn't feeling too good. He's been vomiting but Millie thinks that might have something to do with a heavy night on the turps. The other one has sore ribs, maybe a fracture, so he's finding it painful to breathe.'

'Sounds like a mess.'

'I'm glad I've got you two along.' Mike flashed a grin over his shoulder at Hannah. 'Not the chief bridesmaid duties you were expecting this morning, eh? Sorry about that.'

Hannah smiled back. 'Actually, this is probably more within my comfort zone.'

'We'll have back-up pretty fast. There'll be an ambulance not far behind us and they'll send another one as soon as they're clear. We just need to do the initial triage and make sure they're stable for transport. Couldn't ask for more than two ED specialists on my team.'

'Let's hope it's not as bad as it sounds,' Ryan said. 'At least the rain's slowing down.'

'I've put in a good word to try and get some sunshine for Em this afternoon.'

Ryan laughed. 'You think the big guy's going to listen to you?'

'Hey, I've collected a few brownie points in my time. At least as many as you. Or maybe not.' Mike glanced at his friend. 'How's your dad doing?'

'Not so great. It's hard on Mum.'

'She must be delighted to have you in Auckland now.'

'Yeah.'

'Few trips to Brisbane still on the agenda, though, I guess? How's Michaela?'

Ryan shrugged. 'You know how it is,' was all he said.

'Yeah, buddy.' Mike's response was almost too quiet for Hannah to catch. 'I know.'

What was wrong with Ryan's father? And who was Michaela? An ex-wife? Hannah slumped back a little in her seat. How ridiculous to feel jealous. A timely reminder that this was just one weekend of her life; she didn't need to get caught up in Ryan Fisher's personal business. That was the road to the kind of emotional disaster Hannah had carefully avoided in her life thus far.

Caught up in her own thoughts and then a text conversation with Susie, who had heard about the drama at Wygera and was happy to wait for Emily to collect her, it seemed only a short time later that a tall water tower came into view. The cluster of houses nearby had a sad, tired air to them, with the rusting car bodies on the sparse greenery of surrounding land adding to an impression of poverty.

The eucalyptus trees were huge. They had

been here far longer than the housing and would no doubt outlast most of these dwellings. Right now, the majestic trees were dipping and swaying in the strong wind, participating enthusiastically in a form of elemental ballet. Small branches were breaking free, swirling through the air to join the tumble of leaves and other debris on the bare ground. A larger branch caught Ryan's attention as it landed on the steep roof of the tidiest building they'd seen so far.

'It's the local hall,' Mike told him. 'Built to withstand snow, from what I've heard.' He grinned. 'Really useful, huh? It should manage the odd branch or two, anyway. We've got a turn-off up here and then we should almost be at Rob's place.'

A young woman could be seen waving frantically as they turned onto a rough, unsealed road.

'Target sighted,' Mike said. 'One windmill!'

Hannah was amazed he could sound so relaxed. And that Ryan could share a moment of amusement. She felt completely out of her depth here. They had one paramedic kit between the three of them and three potentially seriously injured teenagers. Hannah had never worked outside a well-equipped emergency department before.

'Hell, you took a long time,' the young woman told them. 'The boys are hurt bad, you know.' She led the way into the house. 'Stupid bulls,' she added with feeling.

'They weren't being nasty,' an older woman said. 'They were scared by the wind and that flapping metal on the shed. Hi, Mike!'

'Hi, Millie.' Mike smiled at the health worker and then at a man who was holding bloodstained towels to the leg of a boy on the couch. 'G'day, Rob. How's it going?'

'I'll let you tell me,' Rob said. His weathered face was creased with anxiety. 'I think I've finally managed to stop the bleeding in Jimmy's leg now, anyway. I've been sitting on the damn thing for an hour.'

Mike had set his backpack-style kit down on the floor and was unzipping it to pull out a stethoscope. 'This is Ryan,' he said, 'and that's Hannah. They're both doctors.' He glanced at the two other boys, who were sitting on the floor, leaning against the wall. They both had a rug over their legs and they both looked miserable.

One had a plastic basin beside him. He shifted his gaze to Millie questioningly.

'Hal's got the sore ribs and Shane's got the puncture wound.' She smiled at Hannah and Ryan. 'Guess you've all got one patient each. Who wants who?'

Hannah swallowed a little nervously. An abdominal goring from a long bull's horn could have resulted in nasty internal injuries that would be impossible to treat in the field. Broken ribs could result in a tension pneumothorax and there were no X-ray facilities to help with diagnosis. A cut leg seemed the safest option. Even if Jimmy had lost enough blood to be going into shock, the treatment was easy. Stop the bleeding, replace fluid and supply oxygen.

'I'll have a look at Jimmy,' she said quickly. 'Have you got a sphygmomanometer in that kit, Mike?'

'Yep.' Mike pulled it out. 'You want to check Shane, Ryan?'

'Sure.'

'Mary?' Mike spoke to the girl who'd shown them inside. 'Could you go back to the road, please? There should be an ambulance arriving before too long and it was really helpful to have you show us where to stop.'

'But I wanted to watch,' Mary protested. 'Are you going to sew Jimmy's leg up?'

'Probably not,' Hannah responded. 'Not until we get him to hospital anyway.'

'Do as you're told,' Millie added firmly.

Hannah moved towards Jimmy, who looked to be about fourteen. 'Hi.'

The youth stared back silently for just a second before averting his eyes, which gave Hannah the impression he'd taken an instant dislike to her.

'I'm going to be looking after you for a bit, Jimmy,' she said. 'Have you ever had your blood pressure taken?'

He shook his head, still avoiding eye contact.

'It doesn't hurt. I'm going to wrap this cuff around your arm. It'll get a bit tight in a minute.'

Ryan had gone to Shane who looked younger than the other two. He was holding a teatowel to his side and it, too, was blood soaked.

Hannah unwound the blood-pressure cuff from Jimmy's arm. His baseline recording for blood pressure was within normal limits but he was young enough to be compensating well for blood loss. She would need to keep monitoring it at regular intervals.

'I'm going to put a small needle in the back of your hand,' she warned Jimmy. 'OK?'

'Why?'

'You've lost a fair bit of blood. We need to give you some fluid to get the volume back up. Blood doesn't work as well as it should if there isn't enough of it going round. Is your leg hurting?'

'Yeah, course it is. It's bloody near chopped off.'

'Can you wiggle your toes?'

'Yeah.' The tone was grudging and Jimmy still wouldn't make eye contact. Was it just her or were all strangers not welcomed by these teens?

'I don't think it's in too much danger of dropping off, Jimmy, ' she said calmly. 'I'll check it properly in a minute. When I've got this needle in your hand, I'll be able to give you something to stop it hurting so much.'

Ryan seemed to be getting a similar suspicious response for being a stranger. Shane didn't look too happy when he put his hand out to touch the teatowel.

'Mind if I have a look, buddy?'

'Are yous really a doctor?'

'Sure am. Just visiting from New Zealand.'

'He's a mate of mine,' Mike told the boys. 'He's going to be the best man at my wedding.'

'Oh, that's right!' Millie exclaimed. 'You're getting married today, Mike. Crikey, I hope you're not going to be late for your own wedding. Dr Emily would be a bit cheesed off.'

'We'll get sorted here in no time,' Mike said calmly. 'Hal, I'm just going to listen to your chest while you take a few breaths, OK?'

'But it hurts.'

'I know, mate. I want to make sure those ribs haven't done any damage to your lung, though. Try to lean forward a bit.'

Hannah had the IV line secured and a bag of fluids attached and running. She got Rob to hold the bag. Having been given the kudos of being Mike's best friend, Ryan now had a more co-operative patient.

'Does it hurt if you take a deep breath?'

'Yeah.'

'Can I have a look at it?'

'I guess.'

'Wow, that's a pretty impressive hole! These bulls must be big fellas.'

'Yeah.'

'Does it hurt if I touch here?'

'Nah. Not much.'

For the next few minutes a rather tense silence fell as they all worked on assessing and treating their patients. Hannah didn't want to disturb the makeshift dressing on Jimmy's leg in case the bleeding started again, but she made a careful examination of his lower leg and foot to check for any serious damage to blood supply and nerves.

Mike was worried about a possible pneumothorax from Hal's broken ribs and got Ryan to double-check his evaluation.

'I think you're right,' Ryan said. 'Breath sounds are definitely down on the left side but it's not showing any signs of tensioning. One of us should travel with him in the ambulance, though.'

The need for constant monitoring and the potential for serious complications from the injury went unspoken, but Hannah could feel the level of tension in the room creep up several notches.

Ryan glanced around him. 'Anyone heard the

one about the blonde and the bulls with big horns?'

Hannah almost groaned aloud. Just when she'd been impressed by the professional, *serious* manner in which Ryan was approaching a job that should have been as much out of his comfort zone as it was for her, he was about to revert to type and tell one of his stupid jokes. Make light of a serious situation.

And then she caught Ryan's gaze.

This was deliberate. He knew exactly what he was doing. This was a ploy—as much of a skill as applying pressure to stop heavy bleeding, only it was intended to work in the opposite direction. A safety valve to relieve pressure. A way of defusing an atmosphere that could be detrimental if it was allowed to continue.

What if Hal picked up on how dangerous a pneumothorax could be and got frightened? He would start to breathe faster, which would not only hurt but interfere with his oxygen uptake. Shane might start vomiting again and exacerbate an internal injury. Jimmy might get restless and open the wound on his leg, with further blood loss.

They were all listening already.

'So, she tells him exactly how many bulls there are in this huge paddock and demands that he honours his side of the bargain and gives her the cute baby one.'

If this was a practised skill, as that almost defensive glance had suggested, what did that tell her about the man Ryan *really* was? Was the fun-loving, laid-back image simply a veneer?

'And the farmer says, "If I can tell you the real colour of your hair, will you give me back my baby bull?"'

Maybe the times Hannah saw Ryan so focussed on his patients—as he had been with Brendon's mother on Monday night and with Shane only minutes ago—said more about who he really was. Or the concern she'd heard in his voice when he'd asked if she was OK on the trip up here. Or…that incredible ability to be so gentle she'd discovered in his touch last night.

No. Hannah couldn't afford to believe in the serious side Ryan was capable of presenting. That was the short cut to disaster that her mother and sister had followed so willingly. She was stronger than that. She could push it away. It was easy, really. All she had to do was remember the way he flirted. The way women flocked to queue up for a chance to go out with him.

He might have the ability to be serious but it couldn't be trusted to last. Serious stuff couldn't be allowed to continue for too long. It just had to be broken by the injection of fun.

'"Now…give me back my dog!"'

Even though she'd only been half listening, Hannah found herself smiling. Shane and Jimmy were giggling. Hal groaned because it hurt, trying to laugh, but he still managed a big grin. Rob and Millie were still laughing when two ambulance officers came through the door with Mary. Eyebrows shot up.

'We heard there was an accident here,' one of them said, 'not a party!'

How many doctors would be able to achieve that? Hannah wondered. Then her own smile broadened. How many doctors had such a supply of awful jokes that could seemingly be adapted to suit the situation? As a demonstration of how useful it could be to be so laid back, this had been an eye-opener. The tension that had filled this room when Hannah had arrived and had threatened to get worse later had gone. Much of the anxiety had left the faces of Rob and Millie and even the boys were all still grinning, even when faced with imminent transport to hospital.

It didn't take long to sort out the transport arrangements. Mike would travel in the ambulance with Hal and Jimmy. Shane demanded to travel with Ryan in the Jeep.

'You can't do that,' Millie said. 'You'd better wait for the other ambulance. You've got a hole in your guts.'

'It's pretty superficial, luckily,' Ryan told her. 'It's going to need a good clean-out and examination under local, but I don't see any harm in Shane riding in the Jeep to start with, anyway. We can meet the other ambulance on the road and transfer him then.'

'Guess that'll be quicker.' Millie waved at Mike as he climbed into the back of the ambulance. 'You'd better get back in time to get your glad rags on, eh?'

Hannah was in the backseat of the Jeep again and Ryan kept up an easy conversation with Shane, interspersed with the occasional query and frequent glance that let Hannah know how closely he was monitoring the lad's condition.

They got back to Crocodile Creek before a rendezvous with the second ambulance. Hannah gave herself a mental shake when she realised that she was disappointed. It wouldn't do to be shut in the confines of a vehicle with no company other than Ryan's, she told herself firmly. It would make it impossible not to feel the strength of the connection that daylight and even a semi-professional working environment had failed to dent.

Disturbingly, it seemed to have become stronger. Hannah stood back in the emergency department of Crocodile Creek Hospital after doing a handover for Jimmy. When Ryan finished transferring the care of Shane to the hospital staff, he turned to look for her. When he spotted her, standing near the water cooler, he smiled.

A different sort of smile. It went with a questioning expression that suggested he really cared about whether she was OK. Like his tone had been when he'd given her his jacket to keep her warm. It touched something deep inside Hannah and made it impossible not to feel happy.

Dangerous, dangerous territory.

She wasn't going to fall in love with Ryan Fisher.

Hannah simply wasn't going to allow it to happen.

CHAPTER SEVEN

WHEN had it happened?

How had it happened?

It wasn't just the atmosphere. The way Mike and Emily were looking at each other as they walked around the altar, taking their first steps as man and wife. Or the chanting of the priest as he gave them his blessing. Or the collective sigh of approval coming from the packed church pews.

There was no question it *had* happened, however.

With her arms full of the white silk train of Emily's dress and the soft tulle of her veil, Hannah was walking very slowly, her arm touching Ryan's as he held the silk ribbons joining the wreaths on the heads of the bridal couple. They got a little tangled at the last corner and there was a momentary pause.

And Ryan looked at her.

There could be no mistaking that sensation of free-fall. The feeling that all the cells in her body were charged with some kind of static electricity and were desperately seeking a focus for their energy.

Or that the focus was to be found in the depths of the dark eyes that were so close to her own. This was a connection that transcended anything remotely physical. The caress of that eye contact lasted only a heartbeat but Hannah knew it would haunt her for life.

It was a moment of truth.

A truth she hadn't expected.

One she most certainly didn't want.

She was in love with Ryan Fisher. She could… incredibly…imagine that this was a ceremony to join *them* in matrimony, not Mike and Emily and the notion only increased that delicious sensation.

Fortunately, Hannah had a huge armful of fabric she could clutch. It brought back memories of the cuddly blanket Susie had dragged around with her for years as a small child, much to Hannah's disgust. The fleecy square had become smaller and smaller over the years and was finally abandoned but somehow the last piece had emerged just after their father had died and Susie had slept with it under her pillow and had genuinely seemed to derive comfort from the limp rag.

Hannah had never needed an inanimate object for comfort.

Until now.

How stupid had it been to go to bed with Ryan?

She *knew* she didn't do one-night stands. She had always believed that that kind of intimacy should be reserved for a relationship that meant something because it was too hard to separate physical and emotional involvement.

Had her subconscious tricked her into believing that, for once, she could do just that? Or had she known all along that her attraction to Ryan had only needed a push to become something far deeper and she had been drawn towards it as inevitably as her mother and sister had been drawn to involvement with the Richards? Had she despised his flirting because, deep down, she had been jealous?

Stupid, stupid, stupid!

How horrified would Ryan be if he guessed how she was feeling? Or, worse, would he take advantage of it, in the Richards style, making the most of having some female fall at his feet—just until he got bored and moved on to a more exciting playground?

Any of those wayward thoughts, generated by the chaos and excitement of the afternoon's preparation for this ceremony, of allowing her one-night stand to become a one-weekend stand had to be squashed.

This had all the makings of a painful ending already. If even a tiny bit more was added to the way Hannah was feeling, it could be just as disastrous as spending weeks or months in a relationship, only to have it end. She might have had no intention of making an emotional investment but something had been automatically deducted from her account without her realising.

Hannah liked that analogy. It wasn't possible to withdraw the sum but she could, at least, stop throwing good money after bad and pull the plug.

Firmly enough to break the chain so she could throw it away.

Facing the congregation as they made their final circuit, Hannah looked up, finally confident she had control again. There was a woman in the second row in the most extraordinary hat she had ever seen. A vast purple creation with bright pink artificial flowers, like giant gerberas, around its brim.

In front of the hat sat Mike's mother, a handkerchief pressed to her face to mop up her tears of joy. His father was using his sleeve to wipe his. Beside them sat a little row of children—the pageboys and flower girls who had done a wonderful job of petal-strewing and had had to sit quietly for the more serious part of the proceedings.

As a sensible insurance policy, Susie sat at the end of the pew, hemming the children in, her crutches propped in front of her, and beside her, in the aisle, was Charles in his wheelchair with one of the flower girls sitting on his lap. The adults were both smiling happily but there was an almost wistful element in both their expressions.

It *had* been a gorgeous service. Sophia must be thrilled that everything had gone so perfectly despite the worry that the worsening weather that afternoon had caused.

Not that any of the bridal party had had time to fret. Kylie, the gum-chewing, self-confessed gossip queen, had worked like a Trojan to make them all as beautiful as possible. Hannah had been startled by how she looked with her soft, natural curls bouncing on her shoulders and more make-up than she would normally have worn. By the time she was encased in her peach silk, sheath dress with the big flower at the base of a plunging halter neckline that matched the explosion of froth at knee level and the sleeveless, silver bolero jacket, Hannah felt almost as gorgeous as Emily looked in her cloud of white lace and flowers.

The men had peach silk bow ties to match the bridesmaids' dresses and silver waistcoats to match their jackets. Hannah hadn't been wrong in thinking they would look irresistibly handsome in their dark suits and white dress shirts. And Ryan, of course, was the best looking of the lot, with his long, lean frame encased in tailored elegance and his dark hair groomed to keep the waves in place. Even a very recent shave hadn't been enough to remove the dark shadow, however, and Hannah couldn't help remembering the scratch of his face that morning on some very tender areas of her skin.

With some difficulty, she dragged her thoughts back to the present. Yes. It had been an over-the-top, fairy-tale wedding ceremony for two people who were obviously very deeply in love and that had the potential to make any single person like Susie or Charles Wetherby reflect on what was missing from their own lives.

It had to be contributing a lot to Hannah's own heightened emotional state. With a bit of luck, she would see things quite differently once they were away from the church.

It was nearly time for the bridal procession. Hannah could see Charles moving his wheelchair and Susie whispering to the children to give them their instructions. They would come at the end of the procession after each pair of bridesmaids and their male counterparts had moved into the aisle. Hannah's partner was, of course, Ryan. She would have to take his arm at least until they got to the foyer, where she would need both hands to help Emily with her veil.

It might take all twelve available bridesmaids' hands, judging by the howl of the wind that could now be heard over the trumpet music. The blast of air inside that came as someone opened the main door of the church was enough to catch Emily's veil and threaten to tear it from her head. The chandelier overhead rattled alarmingly and a crashing sound brought a gasp from everybody standing to watch the procession.

People were craning their necks to see what had happened but they were staring in different directions.

'It was the flowers!' someone near Hannah exclaimed. 'Look!'

Hannah looked. She could see the huge vase of exquisitely arranged peach and white blooms that had toppled from its pedestal near the altar. A large puddle was spreading out from the mound of scattered blooms amongst the shards of broken china.

'No, it came from outside,' someone else shouted. 'Everybody, sit down!'

The priest was looking as alarmed as his congregation. Hannah caught a glimpse of Sophia crossing herself as the priest hurried down the side aisle. Another loud splintering noise was heard as he reached the foyer and his robes were whipping around his legs.

'Close the door,' they heard him order. He

came back to where Emily and Mike had halted a few seconds later. 'There are slates coming off the roof,' he reported. 'You can't go out that way.'

A buzz of consternation rippled through the crowded pews. What was happening? Was this a bad omen for the bridal couple? The noise level continued to increase as the priest spoke to Mike and Emily, pointing towards another door at one side of the church.

'You'll have to go out through the vestry. It's not safe this way.'

'No, no, no!' Sophia was powering down the side aisle, gesticulating wildly. Hannah saw a pretty young woman in a dark blue dress with a matching ribbon in her curly hair get up hurriedly to follow her. 'They can't go backwards,' Sophia cried. 'It's bad luck!'

A chorus of assent came from the congregation nearby. The priest was looking deeply concerned and even Mike and Emily exchanged worried glances.

'How about "take two"?' Ryan suggested calmly. 'We'll push rewind. You guys go back to the altar, have another snog and then go down the side and out the vestry door. That way, you won't be going backwards before you leave the church.'

'How about it, Ma?'

'It's a great idea,' the young woman beside Sophia said firmly. 'Isn't it, Mrs P.?'

'I don't know. I really don't know. This is bad….'

'Don't cry, Ma,' Mike ordered. 'Have you got a spare hanky there, Grace?'

The sound of more slates crashing into the courtyard decided the matter. As one body, the bridal party turned and moved swiftly back towards the altar. The sound of spitting for luck from everybody at the end of the pews was clearly audible despite continuing, excited conversation.

'Hey!' Ryan leaned towards Hannah. 'Aren't you supposed to be hanging on my arm?'

'I don't think we rehearsed this bit.' But Hannah obligingly took the arm being offered.

'I haven't had a chance to tell you but you look fabulous in pink.'

'It's peach, not pink.'

The second kiss that Mike and Emily shared in front of the altar was a little more hurried than the first. They were all aware of the priest now standing by the vestry door, virtually wringing his hands with anxiety. He wanted his church emptied, preferably without anyone being decapitated by flying slates.

Sophia looked as though she would benefit from smelling salts. Unplanned happenings were threatening to disrupt the most carefully orchestrated wedding that Crocodile Creek was likely to experience.

The loose slates weren't the only surprise. Hannah was close behind the bride and groom as the priest opened the vestry door and there, in front of them, was a couple locked in a rather passionate embrace.

It had to be that girl, Georgie, she had seen at the airport. Hannah would have recognised those red stiletto shoes anywhere.

Ryan nudged her. 'Isn't that Alistair—that American neurosurgeon?'

'Yes, I think so.'

'Seems like they've been having their own little ceremony.'

'Mmm.' What was it about this place? Something in the tropical air? Romance seemed to be around every corner.

Maybe *that* was the problem. She'd get over Ryan in a flash once she was breathing nice clean, sensible New Zealand air again. Not that there was time to think even that far into the future. Some of the male guests had braved the front entrance to make sure it was safe to leave the church from this side. Vehicles were being brought right to the door and the mammoth task of shifting the whole congregation to the Athina for the reception was under way.

Any hint of blue patches between the boiling clouds had long gone. It looked as though another heavy, squally rain shower was imminent.

'Quickly, quickly,' Sophia said to everyone passing her at the door. She had clearly abandoned her carefully thought-out transport arrangements and was planning to move everybody as fast as possible. 'We must get home!'

She made Emily, Mike, Ryan, Hannah and Susie squeeze into the first of the limousines. 'The bride mustn't get wet!' she warned. 'It's bad luck!'

Sophia spat three times as Emily and Mike climbed into the spacious rear of the car. What with the huge wedding dress and then Susie's crutches, there wasn't much room left for Ryan and Hannah. They ended up on the same side as Susie with Hannah in the middle. A crutch pressed against her thigh on one side but that discomfort paled in comparison to the disturbing effect of having such close contact with Ryan's thigh on the other side.

'Well, that was fun.' Mike had a huge grin on his face. Then he turned to Emily and his smile faded before he kissed her tenderly.

'Don't mind us,' Ryan drawled.

Mike surfaced reluctantly. 'You should try this some time, mate. It's not that bad.'

'Mmm.' Ryan's sidelong glance at Hannah involved a subtle quirk of an eyebrow. *I know*, the glance said. *I've enjoyed that particular pastime quite recently myself.*

'Hey!' Mike was grinning again. 'If you got around to it soon enough, we could give these suits another airing. I'll return the favour and be *your* best man.'

'I'll keep that in mind.'

Why did Ryan choose that moment to slide his hand under the peachy froth of Hannah's skirt to find her hand? To hold it and give a conspiratorial kind of squeeze?

Had he got some crazy notion himself during that ceremony—as she had? Was Hannah going to be tricked into believing she was a candidate for his bride?

No!

She pulled her hand free but the gesture lost any significance because the driver of the limousine chose precisely that moment to slam on his brakes and she, Ryan and Susie tumbled forward.

'Ouch!' Susie cried.

'Are you all right?' Ryan helped her back onto the leather seat.

Mike slid the glass partition behind his head open. 'What's going on?'

'Rubbish bag flying around in this wind,' the driver told him. 'Sorry—but it landed on the windscreen and I couldn't see a thing. You guys OK back there?'

'Fine,' they all chorused.

Including Hannah. She *was* fine now that Ryan wasn't holding her hand. Now that they'd all been shaken out of the romantic stupor emanating from the bridal couple.

'Crikey!' The car slowed again as it crossed the

old wooden bridge into the cove. 'If that water comes up any more, this'll get washed out to sea.'

The creek was more like a raging torrent and the wind was whipping up small waves on its swift-moving surface. The strings of fairy-lights adorning the exterior of the Athina were seriously challenging the staples holding them in place and Mike heroically gathered Emily's dress together to scoop his bride into his arms and carry her the short distance from the car to the restaurant doors.

Huge, fat drops of rain were starting to fall but Mike moved fast enough to prevent Emily's dress getting damp.

'Thank goodness for that.' She laughed. 'Sophia will be feeling my dress the moment she walks in.'

'Let me check.' Mike ran his hands down the embroidered bodice of the dress and then yanked Emily close. Laughing again, she wrapped her arms around his neck and lifted her face for a kiss.

Ryan's voice was close to Hannah's ear. Too close.

'They have a good rapport, don't they? Just like us.'

Hannah swallowed hard. Even his voice was enough to stir desire. A sharp yearning that was painful because she couldn't allow herself to respond.

'Later,' Ryan murmured. The word was spoken too softly for anyone else to overhear.

'*No!*'

She hadn't expected her response to come out with such vehemence but the promise Ryan's word had contained was too much. *Pull the plug,* her brain was screaming. *Now!*

The momentary freezing on Ryan's part was strong enough for Hannah to sense his shock at the rebuttal but there was no time to try and soften the rejection with any kind of explanation or excuse. The second and third cars from the church had pulled up and Mike's parents spilled out, along with several more clouds of peach-tulled women and dark-suited men.

'Your dress!' Sophia wailed. 'Let me feel your dress, darling! Is it wet?'

'No, it's completely dry. See?' Emily did a twirl in front of the mass of wedding presents piled up in the restaurant entrance.

Mike's father, George Poulos, beamed happily.

'Inside. Everybody inside. Our guests are arriving. It's time to eat, drink and be merry!'

The next hour was a blur of posing for the photographer and then introductions amongst a loud, happy crowd who were determined to ignore the shocking conditions outside. The howl of the wind, the intermittent thunder of rain on the roof and the crash of huge waves on the beach below the restaurant windows were largely drowned out by the enthusiastic live band and even more enthusiastic guests.

Hannah did her best to ignore the rather dark glances that were coming her way from Ryan. It was easy to avoid him by talking to other people. Like Grace, the young nurse with the blue ribbon in her hair.

'It's been my job to try and keep Mrs P. calm,' she told Hannah. Blue eyes that matched her ribbon rolled in mock exasperation. 'As if! Don't be at all surprised if there are a few doves flying around in here later.'

'Plates!' Mike's father carried a stack past them, weaving through a circle of dancers. 'For later,' he threw over his shoulder at Hannah and Grace. 'Don't tell Sophia.'

'I'd better distract her. Excuse me.' Grace hurried away.

'*Opa!*' someone shouted.

A chorus of echoes rippled through the room and Hannah saw a lot of small glasses being raised to lips.

'Ouzo?' A waiter had a tray of the small glasses, as well as the more traditional champagne flutes.

'Maybe later.' Hannah was having trouble trying to keep her head clear enough to remember all the names and she knew she would have to keep it clear to deal with the conversation that was bound to occur with Ryan.

He was right behind the waiter. 'What did you mean, "No"? "No", what?'

'I meant "no" to later,' she said with a resigned sigh.

'But I thought…is something wrong, Hannah?'

'Not at all.' Hannah smiled—reassuringly, she hoped. She would have to work with Ryan. She didn't want to offend him. 'Last night was lovely. Great fun.'

'*Fun?*' Ryan was staring at her. He had no

right to look so shocked. Surely *he* did this kind of thing all the time? A bit of fun. Move on.

'This is Harry.' Grace had returned to where Hannah was standing, staring dumbly back at Ryan. 'He's our local policeman here in the cove. Hi.' She smiled at Ryan. 'You did a good job as best man.'

'I do an even better job at dancing.' Ryan's killer smile flashed as he extended his hand. 'Come on, let me show you.'

It was a snub, Hannah realised as Ryan turned away with Grace on his arm without a backwards glance. He *was* offended for some reason.

Harry was staring after the couple as though he didn't approve any more than Hannah did, but then they managed to smile at each other. In fact, it wasn't that difficult for Hannah to smile. A glow of something like pleasure curled within her. He had liked being with her, then. It had been good enough for him to want more.

If she wasn't so weak, she would have wanted it herself. How wonderful would it be to sink into a relationship with someone like Ryan and enjoy it for what it was? An interlude. One that would set the standard for the best that sex and probably companionship could offer. But to do it without losing too much of her heart and soul?

Impossible.

He would wreck her life eventually.

She would end up like her mother, settling for something that was better than nothing. Learning to enjoy fishing.

Or alone, like Susie, unable to find anyone that excited her as much as the first man who had really stolen her heart.

Harry was telling her something. Hannah made an effort to focus on the tall, good-looking man with a flop of black hair and a worried expression.

'I'm trying to keep tabs on what's happening with Willie,' he told her. 'They're making noises about upgrading it from a category 3 to a 4.'

'Is that serious?'

Harry nodded. 'Cyclones are all dangerous. 'Specially Aussie ones—they're known for exhibiting a more erratic path than cyclones in other parts of the world. The higher the number, the more danger they represent. A category 3 is a severe tropical cyclone. You can get wind gusts up to 224 kilometres per hour and can expect roof and structural damage, and a likely power failure.'

'The slates were certainly flying off the church.'

'There's a few people with tarps on their roofs already. They'll lose them if things get any worse.'

'And they're expected to?'

'It's been upgraded to a 4. It's running parallel to the coast at the moment but if it turns west we'll be in trouble. A 4 has winds up to 279 kilometres per hour. You'll get significant structural damage, dangerous airborne debris and widespread power failures.'

As though to underline Harry's sombre tone, the lights inside the Athina flickered, but there was still enough daylight for it not to matter and they came back on almost immediately.

'I'm with the SES—State Emergency Services,' Harry finished. 'In fact, if you'll excuse me, I should make a call and see what's happening.'

Just as Harry disappeared, Ryan emerged from an animated group of Greek women nearby.

'Fun?' he queried with quiet menace. 'Is that all it was for you, Hannah? *Fun?'*

This was disconcerting. She would have expected a shrugged response from Ryan by now. A 'there's plenty more fish in the sea' kind of attitude.

'It *was* fun.' She tried to smile. To break the tension. 'But we both know it could never be any more than that.'

'*Do* we?' Ryan held her gaze. Challenging her. 'Why is that?'

'Oh, come on, Ryan.' Hannah looked for an escape. Someone to talk to. A new introduction. Where was Susie when she needed her? Nothing seemed readily available. They were marooned. A little island of hostility that was keeping all the happy people away with an invisible force field. 'We're not on the same page, remember?'

'Obviously not,' Ryan snapped. 'There I was thinking that we had made a fresh start. The start of something that could actually be meaningful.'

Meaningful? Oh, help! It would be so easy to believe that. Hannah so *wanted* to believe it. To believe *she* could be the one to tame this particular 'bad boy'. To have him love her so much he would be content to settle down and never get bored.

The wheelchair arrived beside them so smoothly neither had noticed.

'I'm Charles Wetherby,' the man said unnecessarily. 'I must apologise for this awful weather Crocodile Creek is turning on for you. I hope you're still managing to enjoy yourselves.'

Hannah had the weird feeling that Charles had known exactly how much they were enjoying themselves and was there to do something to defuse the atmosphere.

Ryan controlled the flash of an ironic smile and managed to introduce both himself and Hannah to Charles without missing a beat.

And then he excused himself, as though he couldn't stand being in Hannah's company any longer.

He was hurt, she realised. She hadn't expected that at all. It was confusing. Why would he be hurt...unless he was being honest. Unless he really had thought there was something meaningful going on.

No. He might think that—for now. He might even believe it long enough for Hannah to trust it, but he was a type, wasn't he? He was, what, in his mid-thirties? At least a couple of years older than she was, given his professional experience. If he was into commitment he wouldn't still be playing the field. And what about

Michaela? Was she someone who had believed in him and had now been discarded?

Hannah had to paste a smile onto her face to talk to Charles.

'You look so like Susie,' he was saying. 'It's a real treat. Must be wonderful to have a sibling that you're so close to.'

'It is.'

'Uncle Charles! Look at me! I'm dancing!'

The small blonde flower girl who had been sitting on Charles's knee during the ceremony was part of a circle of dancers, between two adults. She wasn't watching the steps any more because her head was twisted in Hannah's direction and she had a huge smile on her face.

'This way, Lily.' Mike's sister, Maria, had hold of one of Lily's hands. 'We go this way now.'

'*Opa!*' The cry to signal a new round of toasting the bridal couple rang out.

'Ouzo?'

'No, thanks.' Hannah shook her head at the attentive waiter. Lily had given her an excuse to watch the dancers and Ryan was now part of the circle. So was Mike. And then the circle disintegrated as Sophia bustled through.

'Eat! Eat! The food will be getting cold.'

Ryan and Mike took no notice. With an arm around each other's shoulders and their other arms extended, they were stepping in a dance of their own. Happy. Relaxed. The bond of a deep friendship was obvious to everyone and they all approved. They were clapping and stamping their feet in time with the music and calling encouragement.

And then George was on the dance floor, a plate in each hand.

'No!' Sophia cried.

But the sound of smashing crockery only brought a roar of approval and more people back to the dance floor.

Hannah turned away. She spotted Susie sitting with a very pregnant woman. They had plates of food from the buffet.

Not that Hannah felt hungry. Watching Mike and Ryan dance had left her with a curious sense of loss. How long had Ryan known his best friend? Ten years? More? Their bond appeared unshakable. Mike trusted him completely.

But Mike wasn't a woman. The ending of a friendship, however close, could never destroy someone as much as the ending of the most intimate relationship it was possible to have.

It was really quite straightforward so why was her heart winning the battle with her head right now?

Why did she feel this sense of loss? As though she had just made a terrible mistake?

Because it was already too late. She was in love with this man.

She was already prepared to believe in him.

And if he gave her another chance, she would take it.

Take the risk.

Do whatever it took to spend as much time as possible with him. In bed and out of it.

The rest of her life, even.

CHAPTER EIGHT

THIS had to be the ultimate putdown.

And he had only himself to blame.

It had only been one night. Hannah Jackson was only one of hundreds of women Ryan had met since he'd grown up enough to be interested in the opposite sex. Thousands, even, and he'd dated a fair few in those early years. Slept with enough to know how rare it was to find a woman who could be both intellectually and physically stimulating.

He could have dealt with that attraction, however powerful it had been, when that was all it was. Moved on with maybe just a shrug of regret. But Hannah had taken down that barrier. Taken him by the hand and shown him a place he had never been to before. A place he didn't want to leave.

And now she was shoving him out. Had put that barrier back up and….it *hurt,* dammit!

Nobody had ever treated him like this before—and she'd accused *him* of being shallow? What reason did she have? She might have been hurt in the past, he reminded himself. Some bastard might have treated her badly enough to leave scars that hadn't healed yet.

No. It didn't matter how good the reason might be. Or how fresh the scars. Why the hell would he set himself up for another kick in the guts like the one she'd just delivered? With a smile, no less. A damning with faint praise.

Fun? Like a night out? A party? A game of tennis?

'What's up, mate?' Mike's fingers dug into his shoulder. 'You look like you're at a funeral, not a wedding.'

'Sorry. Miles away.'

'Not in a happy place, by the look of that scowl. Forget it. Come and eat. The lamb's wonderful and Ma will be force-feeding you soon if she doesn't see you holding a plate.'

'Good idea. And I think a drink or two is overdue as well.'

'Just don't get trollied before you have to make that speech and tell everyone how wonderful I am.'

Ryan laughed. 'More like seeing how many stories of your disreputable past I can dredge up. What time am I on?'

'Just before the cake-cutting. I think Ma's got it down for about 8:30 p.m.'

'Cool. Gives me half an hour to see how much I can remember. What was the name of that girl in Bali? The one with all the tattoos?'

'Don't you dare! You might get Em worried I haven't settled down.'

'And have you?'

'No question, mate. I'll never look at another woman. I've found the one for me. Oh, great— a slow song! Catch you later. Go and eat. I'm hanging out for a waltz with my wife.'

Lucky man, Ryan thought, watching Emily's face light up as Mike reached her and the way she seemed to float dreamily in his arms as they found a space on the dance floor.

Lucky, lucky man.

The lights had flickered more than once in the last hour but this time they went out and stayed out.

Hannah, sitting with Susie, the very pregnant doctor called Christina and her gorgeous, dark-skinned husband Joe, who had turned out to be a fellow New Zealander, had also been watching the bridal couple dance. And Harry and Grace, who were dancing towards the edge of the crowd. And the woman who hadn't taken off that extraordinary purple hat with the huge flowers.

'That's Dora for you,' Susie was saying. 'She's so proud of that hat she'll probably wear it when she's polishing floors at the hospital for the next week or—'

She stopped as the room plunged into semi-darkness. The candles on tables provided only a dim light that would take a few moments to adjust to. People were just shadowy figures. The dancing had stopped and there was an uncertain kind of milling about, both on the dance floor and around the tables. The couple who were not moving at all in the corner caught more than Hannah's attention.

'Who *is* that?' Susie whispered loudly. 'I can't see in this light.'

'Whoever they are, they seem to like each other.' Joe grinned.

Susie winked at Hannah. 'Yeah. I'd say they've got a pretty good rapport all right.'

Hannah elbowed her sister. A reminder of what had started this small life crisis she was experiencing was not welcome.

They found out who the male of the pair was almost immediately, as Charles Wetherby rolled past their table accompanied by a young police officer who was holding a candelabrum. The flames on several candles were being dragged backwards to leave little smoke trails due to the speed with which the men were moving.

'Harry Blake!' The tone was urgent enough for conversation to die amongst everyone within earshot and the reaction to it spread rapidly. A lot of people could hear what Charles had to say as Harry seemed to attempt to shield the woman he'd been kissing so passionately by steering her further into the dark corner and then striding forward to meet the hospital's medical director.

'Bus accident up on the mountain road,' Hannah heard him say.

'I think it was *Grace* he was kissing,' Susie whispered. 'Woo-hoo!'

'Shh!' Hannah warned. 'This sounds serious.'

Joe's chair scraped as he got up and moved towards the knot of men. Christina's bottom lip was caught between her teeth and she laid a protective hand, instinctively, on her swollen belly. Tension and urgency were radiating strongly from their centre of focus.

Everybody who could hear was listening avidly. Others were trying to find out what was being said.

'What's going on?' someone called.

'Why are the police here?'

'Why haven't the lights come back on?'

'The hospital's four-wheel drive is on its way here to pick up whatever hospital staff you think you might need on site. Have you seen Grace? If we've got to set up a triage post and then get people off the side of the mountain, we'll probably need an SES crew up there, as well….'

Mike was heading towards the expanding knot of male figures. So was Ryan. Hannah got to her feet. If this was a major incident, they would need all the medical expertise available.

Charles would be magnificent in any crisis, Hannah decided. So calm. So in touch with what was happening everywhere in his domain.

'We've been on standby to activate a full code black disaster response, thanks to the cyclone watch on Willie,' he told the cluster of medics now around him. 'I'm going to go ahead and push the button. We have no idea how many casualties we might get from this bus but it looks likely we're in for trouble from Willie so it'll give us a few hours' head start. A dry run, if you like.'

'What's happening?' Sophia pushed her way towards Charles. Dora Grubb was not far behind her, the pink flowers on her hat wobbling nervously.

'There's been an accident, Sophia,' Charles said. 'A bus full of people has vanished off the road near Dan Macker's place. Big landslide, thanks to all the rain we've had this week.'

'Oh… *Oh!*' Sophia crossed herself, her face horrified. 'This is bad!'

'I'm going to have to call in all available medical staff, starting with everyone here. Including Mike and Emily. I'm sorry, Sophia.'

'*Oh!*' Sophia looked stricken now. 'But the cake! The speeches!' Then she rallied, visibly pulling herself together. She stood as tall as possible for a short, plump person. 'Of course you need my boy,' she said proudly. 'And our

Emily. Who else can look after those poor people if they need an operation? Emily! Darling! Let me help you find something else to wear.'

Hannah looked down at the froth of peach tulle around her knees and on to the flimsy white shoes with the flowers on the toes.

Mike noticed the direction of her glance. 'I've got spare flight suits in our room and Em's probably got a spare set of boots. Ryan? You'd better come and grab a suit, too.'

'Thanks, mate.'

'At least you won't have to roll up the sleeves and legs. Come with me, you guys. Let's get kitted up.'

It was Susie's turn to look stricken. 'I want to help but I'm useless with these crutches!'

'Not at all,' Charles said. 'You can stay with me and Jill. There's a lot of admin we'll need to do at the hospital. Code black means we've got to empty as many beds as we can. Set up a receiving ward. Mobilise stores. Reorganise ED…'

The list was still continuing as Hannah hurried in the wake of Mike and Ryan. She could also hear Dora Grubb talking excitedly to Sophia.

'They'll need food, all these rescue people.'

'We *have* food. Too much food. All this lamb! I'll tell the chef to start making sandwiches.'

It took less than ten minutes for the four young medics to encase themselves in the helicopter service issue overalls.

Emily sighed as she took a glance over her shoulder at the mound of white lace and silk on the bed. 'It was nice while it lasted,' she said, 'being a princess.'

'You'll always be a princess, babe,' Mike assured her. 'And I reckon you know how sexy I think you look in those overalls.'

Hannah carefully avoided looking anywhere close to Ryan's direction. She could understand the look that passed between Mike and Emily because she had stolen a glance at Ryan moments before, when he'd bent to lace up the spare pair of Mike's heavy steel-capped boots, and there had been no danger of him catching her glance.

It was a completely different look to civvies. Or scrubs. Or the white coat that doctors never seemed to bother with any more. He looked taller, somehow. Braver. Ready to get out there and save lives. And there was a very determined tilt to his chin that she hadn't seen before. Tension that visibly knotted the muscles in his jaw.

Was he anticipating a tough job at the scene of the bus crash or was it controlled anger? Directed at her?

Whatever.

Sexy didn't begin to cover how he looked.

Hannah scraped back her carefully combed curls and wound an elastic band to form a ponytail. Would Ryan see *her* as looking adventurous and exciting in these overalls with the huge rolled-up cuffs on the arms and legs?

Not likely.

Especially as he appeared determined not to actually look directly at her at all.

Even in the back of an ambulance a commendably short time later, when they had collected gear and co-ordinated with other personnel at the hospital, he was avoiding anything as personal as direct eye contact.

Mike was with them. Emily had ended up staying behind at the hospital to oversee the set-up and preparation of Theatres. Because of the weather conditions, with injured people exposed to the rain and wind, she needed to organise fluid warming devices and forced-air warmers on top of making sure she was ready to administer a general anaesthetic at short notice.

A second ambulance was following with another crew and all Crocodile Creek's available fire appliances had gone on ahead. Police had been first on scene, and by the time Hannah arrived, the road was lined with vehicles—a chain of flashing lights they had glimpsed from miles away as they'd sped up the sometimes tortuous curves of the mountain road. Lights that had haloes around them right now thanks to the heavy curtain of rain.

A portable triage tent was erected on the road to one side of the massive obstacle of mud, rocks and vegetation. Guy ropes had it anchored but the inflatable structure was looking alarmingly precarious in the high wind and its sides were being sucked in and then ballooning out almost instantly with a loud snapping sound.

The generators used to fill the outlines of the tent with compressed air were still running, powering lights, including some that were being directed downhill from the point where large skid marks were visible. There was more noise from the fire engines whose crews were rolling out winch cables from the front of the heavy vehicles. Pneumatic tools like the Jaws of Life were being primed and tested. As a background they were already tuning out, the wind howled through the treetops of the dark rainforest around them.

Harry Blake, wearing a fluorescent jacket that designated him as scene commander, met the ambulance, framed by the back doors Mike pushed open and latched.

'Who's in charge?' he queried briskly.

'I'm liaising with the medical director at the ED.' Mike clipped his radio to his belt. 'What frequency are we using on site?'

'Channel 8.'

Mike nodded. 'Channel 6 is the hospital link.' He leapt out of the back of the ambulance. 'I'll go down and triage with these two doctors and then we'll deploy all the other medical crews we get. What's it looking like down there?'

'It's a bloody mess,' Harry said grimly. 'The bus must have come off the road at speed and it rolled on the way down. The windows have popped out and we've got people and belongings all over the place. Some of the seats have come adrift inside and there's people trapped, but we can't get inside until the fire boys get a line or two onto the bus.'

'It's not stable?' Mike was sliding his arms into the straps of his backpack containing medical supplies.

'Hell, no. It could slide farther, especially if it keeps raining like this.'

Hannah and Ryan were out of the ambulance now, standing beside Mike. 'Don't forget your helmets,' he reminded them. Then his attention was back on Harry. 'Any fatalities?'

'At least one.' Harry raised his voice to a shout to be heard as they started walking and got closer to the generators. 'There's a guy who's been thrown clear and then caught under the bus. He's at the front and we think he's probably the driver. We won't be able to shift him until we can jack up the front corner somehow.'

'The fire guys going to be able to use their cutting gear down there? Is it safe to have them clambering around?'

'We've got nets anchored on the slope. It's not

too bad for climbing. There's an SES crew down there at the moment, trying to clear the scene of everybody who's able to move.'

'How many are we dealing with?' Ryan had jammed his hard hat on and was pulling the strap tight.

Harry shook his head. 'Haven't been able to do a head count yet. There's injured people over quite a wide area. We think there's two or three still trapped in the bus, from what we can see. One of the passengers who's not hurt thinks the bus was quite full. There's about ten people we can bring up now. Could be fifteen or twenty still down there needing attention.'

Mike and Ryan shared a glance. This was huge. It was going to stretch their resources and everybody's skills.

'Let's do it.' Ryan pulled on latex examination gloves and then heavier ones for climbing. He gave Mike a thumbs-up and Mike responded with a terse nod and another shared glance. They had faced difficult situations before. They were more than ready to tackle this one. Together.

Hannah felt oddly excluded. Even when Mike

put her after Ryan and before himself to protect her as she climbed down the steep, slippery slope, she didn't really feel a part of this small team.

Ryan hated her. He didn't want her there.

Within the first few metres of their climb, however, any thoughts of personality clashes or anything else that could affect a working relationship were forgotten.

A woman lay, moaning. 'My leg,' she groaned. 'I can't get any further. Help…'

This was an initial triage. No more than thirty seconds could be allocated for any patient to check for life-threatening injuries like uncontrolled haemorrhage or a blocked airway. Mike had triage tags in his pocket. Big, brightly coloured labels with an elastic loop that would alert all other personnel to the priority the victims had for medical attention. This woman was conscious and talking. It took less than thirty seconds for Ryan to examine her.

'Fractured femur. Closed. No external bleeding. Airway's clear.'

Mike produced a yellow label. Attention needed but second priority. 'Someone will be with you as soon as possible,' he reassured the woman as they moved on. 'We've got to check everybody else first and then we'll be back.'

'But it *hurts*…Oh-h-h….'

It was hard, leaving her to keep descending the slope. A huddle of people near the base of the nets were bypassed. They were all mobile and being looked after by SES people. Grace was there, organising the clearance of the less injured from the scene. Mike gave her a handful of green triage tags that designated the lowest priority. Hannah saw a young Asian couple clinging to each other, looking terrified, and she could hear someone talking in a foreign language that sounded European. Had the bus been full of tourists? It could make their job more difficult if they couldn't communicate with their patients.

A young woman lay, unconscious, against the base of a huge eucalyptus tree.

'Hello, can you hear me?' Hannah pinched the woman's ear lobe. 'Non-responsive,' she told Mike. She laid a hand on the woman's neck and another on her belly. 'She's breathing. Good carotid pulse. Tachy.'

The elastic of a pink triage label went over her wrist. Highest priority. This case was urgent,

with the potential to be saved and the likelihood
of rapid deterioration if left. They moved on.

'There's one over here,' a fire officer yelled at
them. 'He's making a weird noise.'

'Occluded airway.' Mike repositioned the
man's head and the gurgling sound ceased.
Another pink tag.

Winch hooks were being attached to the bus.
There were no big lights down here and the
rescue workers had to make do with the lamps
on their helmets. A curious strobe effect to
viewing the disaster was evident as lights
intersected and inspected different areas. It
made it easier to deal with, Hannah decided,
because you could only see a patch at a time.
A single patient, a broken window, dented
metal, broken tree branches, strewn belongings and luggage.

Just the top half of the unfortunate man who
had been caught beneath the front wheel of the
bus. It took only a moment to confirm the extinc-
tion of life and give the man a white tag to
signify a fatality so that nobody would waste
time by checking him again.

'Don't go downhill from the bus.' A fire officer

with a winch hook in his hand shouted the warning. 'We haven't got this thing stable yet.'

The doors of the bus were blocked because it was lying, tilted, on that side. The emergency hatch at the back was open, however, and must have been how some of the less injured had escaped the wreckage.

Mike saw Ryan assessing the access. 'Not yet, buddy,' he said firmly. 'You can just wait until it's safer.'

Safer, Hannah noted. Not *safe.* It could never be really safe to do something like this, could it? And yet Ryan was clearly frustrated by having to hold back.

Hannah shook her head to clear the water streaming down her face from looking up at the hatch. She was soaked now and the wind was chilling. She flexed increasingly stiff fingers and cast a glance at her colleagues.

There was certainly no doubting Ryan's commitment to his work and the people he cared for. How many ED specialists would be prepared to work in conditions like this? To risk their own lives without a moment's hesitation to try and save others?

Mike might have been off the mark in making people think Ryan was some kind of saint, but he hadn't been wrong in advertising him as a hero. They both were. The way these two men worked together suggested they had been in situations before that had not been dissimilar. There was a calm confidence about the way they worked that was contagious.

Like Ryan's courage in that plane turbulence had been.

What if she couldn't redress the antipathy Ryan now held towards her and the one who didn't win that consultancy position in ED felt obliged to go and work elsewhere? If she never had the chance to work with him again?

The sense of loss she had experienced watching him dance with Mike came back strongly enough to distract Hannah for several seconds. Was it always going to haunt her? Did she have to be ruthlessly squashed at frequent intervals in order for her to perform to her best ability? Like now?

Hannah continued the triage exercise with grim determination. They found another five people with fractures and lacerations who needed yellow tags. One more pink tag for a partially amputated arm and severe bleeding. An SES worker had been doing a great job of keeping pressure on the wound. Then they were given the all-clear to check out the bus.

'Not you, Hannah,' Mike stated. 'You can check in with the SES guys. Make sure we haven't missed anyone. Get someone to check further afield as well. We've got debris over a wide area and injured people could have moved or even fallen further down the slope.'

Hannah moved to find someone to talk to but she couldn't help stopping for a moment. Turning back to watch as the two men climbed into the bus.

Turning back again a moment later, when alarmed shouting heralded a noticeable shift in the position of the bus.

'Oh, my God...' Was the bus going to move with the extra weight? Slide and possibly roll again down the side of this mountain?

Remove any possibility of repairing the rift she'd created with Ryan?

Remove Ryan from her life with the ultimate finality of death?

'*No-o-o!*'

It was a quiet, desperate sound, snatched away and disguised by the howl of the wind. If it was a prayer, it was answered. Having taken up some slack from one of the winch cables, the movement stopped. Mike actually leaned out a broken window with his thumb and forefinger forming the 'O' of a signal that they were OK.

It was only then that Hannah realised she had been holding her breath. A couple of minutes later and Ryan and Mike emerged from the bus.

'One pink, one yellow, one white,' Mike reported. 'One's unconscious and another's trapped by a seat.' He reached for his radio. Medical crews could now be co-ordinated, specific tasks allocated, patients treated and evacuated. The most seriously injured patients would be assigned a doctor who would stabilise and then escort them to hospital.

Hannah was joined by a paramedic by the name of Mario, issued a pack of gear and assigned the case of the woman who had been pink-ticketed at the base of the eucalyptus tree. Mike and Ryan were going to work on the pink-ticket patient inside the bus. Hannah watched them climb inside again. A scoop stretcher was passed in along with the pack of resuscitation gear by firemen who then waited, knowing their muscle would be needed to assist with extrication.

Once again Hannah felt that sense of loss as Ryan vanished from view and this time she couldn't quite shake it off.

She *needed* him, dammit! This was so far out of her comfort zone, it wasn't funny. The rain might be easing but she was still soaked and cold and her fingers felt uselessly stiff and clumsy.

The effort to concentrate seemed harder than it had ever been. Hannah was trying to recall the workshop she'd attended at a conference once, on the practice of emergency medicine in a hostile environment. Control of the airway was the first priority, of course, with cervical spine control if appropriate.

It was appropriate in this case. Hannah's gloved hand came away streaked with blood after touching the back of the young woman's head. Had she been thrown clear of the bus and hit the tree she now lay beside? If the blow had been enough to cause her loss of consciousness, it had potentially caused a neck injury as well.

'I need a collar,' she told Mario. She placed her hand, side on, on the woman's shoulder, making a quick estimate of the distance to her jaw line. 'A short neck, please. And a dressing for this head wound.'

It was difficult, trying to assess how well their patient was breathing. Hard to see, given the narrow focus of the beam of light from her helmet. Hard to feel with her cold hands and impossible to hear with the shouting and noise of machinery. And over it all, the savage wind still howled. Large tree branches cracked ominously and small pieces of debris like broken branches flew through the air, occasionally striking Hannah in the back or hitting the hard helmet she wore with a bang, magnified enough to make her jump more than once.

'I don't think we can assess her for equal air entry until we get her into an ambulance, at least,' she said. 'She's certainly breathing on her own without any respiratory distress I can pick up.'

Which was a huge relief. While this woman

was probably unconscious enough to be able to be intubated without a drug regime, the lecturer at that conference had discussed the difficulties of intubation in a situation like this. Often, the technique of cricothyroidotomy was more appropriate and that wasn't something Hannah wanted to attempt with limited light and frozen fingers.

IV access was more manageable. Hannah placed a large-bore cannula in the woman's forearm and started fluids. She remembered to use extra tape to secure both the cannula and the IV fluid lines. The lecturer's jocular warning was what she'd remembered most clearly about that workshop. "If it can fall out," he'd said, 'it *will* fall out.'

Mario had the expertise and strength to move the woman onto a backboard and strap her securely onto it. And then the firemen took over, inching their way up the mountainside with the help of ropes and the net.

Moving to follow them, the beam of Hannah's light caught something that made her stoop. She picked the object up. It was a shoe. A rather well-worn sneaker with a hole in the top and what looked like a picture of a bright orange fish done in felt pen or something similar. What startled her was its size. It was small.

Very small.

A child's shoe.

But they hadn't come across any children in their triage, had they? Hannah had the awful thought that it could be the fatality inside the bus. But maybe the owner of this shoe was un-injured? Not seen amongst that huddle of frightened people who had been waiting for help up the slope? Hannah certainly hoped so. And if they were, they might have one bare foot and be grateful to see that shoe. Hannah stuffed it into the large pocket on the front of her overalls.

It wouldn't have been easy for a child to climb, even with the hand- and footholds the net provided. They were wet now and very muddy. Hannah slipped, more than once, and had to save herself by grabbing the netting or a tree root or branch.

How could fifty metres seem such a long way? And how long had they been on scene? Certainly no more than an hour, but she felt as though she had just completed a full night shift in the ED and a busy one at that.

The third time she slipped, Hannah might well have fallen but she was caught by her arm in a vice-like grip.

'Are you OK?' Ryan asked.

It had to be her imagination that she could hear the same kind of caring in the query that she had heard in the car on the way to Wygera that morning. An aeon ago. In her current state it was enough to bring the sting of tears to her eyes. She blinked them away.

'Yeah…thanks…'

'Not easy, this stuff, is it?' Ryan was climbing beside her. Just below them, the scoop stretcher containing his patient was making slow progress upwards. 'How's your woman?'

'Still unconscious but breathing. A head injury but I have no idea how bad it is yet.'

'You'll be able to do a more thorough assessment in the ambulance. We won't be far behind you if you run into trouble. Mike says they're going to stage departures so we arrive at the ED at about six-minute intervals. Just pull over and keep your lights on and we'll stop to help.'

'Thanks,' Hannah said again. Professional assistance but at least he was talking to her. She was almost at the top of the slope now. A fire officer had his hand out to help her onto the road and the noise level increased markedly. She could still hear Ryan's call, though.

'Hey, Hannah?'

'Yeah?'

'You're doing a fantastic job. Well done.'

Those tears were even closer all of a sudden. They couldn't be allowed to spill. Hannah clenched her fists as she got to her feet on the road and her hand struck her bulky pocket. She peered down at Ryan.

'Hey, did you come across any children in the bus?'

'No. Why?'

'I found a shoe. A kid's size shoe.' She pulled it from her pocket. 'See?'

'Could have come from anywhere,' Ryan said. 'Maybe there's a kid amongst the green tickets.'

'Yes, I thought of that. I'll check with Grace later.'

'It could have come from spilled luggage as well. Or even been thrown away. Looks pretty old.'

'Hannah?' Mario, the paramedic, was calling. She could see the backboard supporting her patient being lifted into the back of an ambulance. 'We're nearly ready to roll.'

'On my way.' Hannah turned to give Ryan a smile of thanks for his help but he wasn't watching. He had already turned back to his patient.

'I'll take over the ventilations there, Mike. You've done a fantastic job up the hill.'

A fantastic job. Like her. So the praise hadn't really been personal, had it? The doors of the ambulance slammed shut behind her and someone thumped on the back to give the officer driving the signal to go. Hannah took a deep breath.

'Let's get some oxygen on, Mario. A non-rebreather mask at ten litres a minute. And I want a slight head tilt on the stretcher. Can we do that with a backboard in the way?'

'Sure, we'll just use a pillow under this end.'

'Let's get some definitive baseline measurements, too. Blood pressure, heart rate and rhythm, oxygen saturation.' She pulled a stethoscope from the kit. 'I'm going to check her breathing again.'

It felt good to be on the move towards a fully equipped emergency department and hospital.

Hannah would feel far more in control then. Far less likely to be thrown off balance by overly emotional reactions to someone else's words or the way they looked at her. Or *didn't* look at her.

It helped to know that Ryan would be on the road within minutes, though. Travelling in the same direction she was. Sharing the same experiences and goals that had arrived in their lives so unexpectedly. To get through this ordeal and help as many people as possible.

They were on the same page now, weren't they?

What a shame it was just too late.

CHAPTER NINE

THE contrast couldn't have been greater.

The Poulos wedding had been a happy circus. Crocodile Creek Base Hospital was hosting a miserable one.

Injured, bewildered people filled the cubicles and sat on chairs. A moving sea of professional staff was doing everything necessary. Doctors, nurses, clerks, radiographers and orderlies were doing their jobs. And more. The fact that it was late at night and the majority of people here were not rostered on duty meant nothing. A disaster response had been activated and there was nobody associated with this medical community who wasn't prepared to do whatever they could to help.

There was a lot to be done. Hannah's case was the first serious one to arrive so she had the initial advantage of all the staff she could possibly need to assist.

Luke hadn't yet gone to the receiving ward where he would be available on the surgical team, along with Cal and Alistair. Emily was still in the department as well, because minor cases needing surgery were going to have to wait until all the majors had been dealt with. They both came to assist Hannah. Charles wasn't far behind.

'You should get changed out of those wet overalls,' he told Hannah. 'There's plenty of people here to take over. Susie can show you where the scrubs are kept.'

'Soon,' Hannah promised. 'I just want to make sure she's stable.' Having come this far with the injured woman, Hannah was reluctant to hand over. 'If that's OK with you, Dr Wetherby?'

Ryan might be registered to work in Australia but Hannah wasn't. It was Charles who could give her permission. It was up to him whether he trusted that she was competent enough not to cause problems he would have to take ultimate responsibility for.

The look she received was assessing but Charles had obviously seen enough to make a decision.

'Go ahead,' he said.

Mario and a male nurse had moved the woman, still strapped to her backboard, onto the bed.

'Right.' Hannah nodded, tucking away the pleasure that someone like Charles Wetherby was prepared to trust her. 'This woman was apparently thrown clear of the bus and was found unconscious. There's been some response on the way in but nothing coherent. I'd put her GCS at seven. She was initially tachycardic at 120 but that's dropped in the last fifteen minutes to a rate of 90, respirations are shallow but air entry is equal and the oxygen saturation has been steady on 97 per cent on 10 litres.'

Standard monitoring equipment was being attached to the woman, like ECG leads, a blood-pressure cuff and an oxygen saturation monitor. Someone was hanging the fluids from a ceiling hook and another nurse was taking the woman's temperature.

'Thirty-five point six degrees centigrade,' she reported.

'Not hypothermic, then,' Emily commented.

'Blood pressure was initially one-twenty on eighty. Last measurement was one-thirty on seventy.'

'Widening pulse pressure,' Luke said. 'Rising intracranial pressure?'

'Quite possible. She has an abrasion and haematoma in the occipital area. No obvious skull fracture. Pupils were equal and reactive.'

'They're not now.' Emily was at the head end of the bed, shining a bright torch into the woman's eyes. 'Right pupil is two millimetres larger and sluggish.'

'Do we know her name?' Luke asked.

'No.' Hannah glanced at one of the nurses. 'Perhaps you could check her pockets? She may have some ID.'

'We need some radiography,' Luke said. 'Preferably a CT scan. And where's Alistair? If we've got a neurosurgeon available, this is where he should be.'

Charles pivoted his wheelchair. 'I'll find him.'

The movement of the woman on the bed was unexpected. Restrained, due to the straps still holding her to the backboard, but unmistakable.

'She's going to vomit,' Emily warned.

'Let's turn her side on,' Hannah ordered. 'I'll need suction.'

It was easy to turn the woman onto her side and keep her spine protected, thanks to the back-board, but it was another sign that the pressure could be building dangerously inside her head.

The nurse checking her pockets had easier access with the patient tipped to one side. 'I've found something,' she said. 'It's a passport. An Australian one.'

'Great. At least she'll understand the language. And we'll be able to use her name.' Hannah glanced up at the monitor, to see what was happening with the blood pressure. 'What is it?'

'Janey Stafford.'

'What?' The startled query came from Luke. 'Did you say *Janey Stafford?*'

'Do you know her?' Hannah asked. It could be helpful for an unconscious person to hear the voice of someone she knew.

'I… I'm not sure.' Luke was looking stunned. He reached over and lifted the oxygen mask the woman had on. Was he looking for a feature he might recognise? Hannah wondered. Like that small mole at the corner of her top lip?

Luke was backing away. Shaking his head.

'You don't know her, then?'

'Not really. It was her sister I knew.' The tone was dismissive. An 'I don't want to talk about this' sort of tone. 'It was a long time ago.'

Emily was staring at Luke. Then she blinked and refocussed. 'Do you want me to intubate?' she asked Hannah.

Alistair walked into the resus bay at that moment.

'I'll hand over to an expert,' Hannah said. Having given Alistair a rundown on their findings so far, she found herself stepping back. Luke did more than step back. He left the resus bay completely.

But then a new emergency was coming in. Luke hadn't pulled the curtain closed behind him and Hannah could see Ryan arriving with his multi-trauma case from the interior of the bus. They were still using a bag mask to ventilate this patient. There were two IV lines in place and Ryan looked worried.

'Bilateral fractured femurs,' Hannah heard him tell Charles. 'Rib fractures and a flail chest. GCS of nine.'

Charles directed them to resus 2 and Luke disappeared behind the curtain along with them.

The picture of Ryan's face was not so quick to disappear for Hannah. She had seen him work under duress before. Seen him tired and even not a hundred per cent well himself, but she had never seen an expression like the one he had walked in with.

So grim. Determined. So…lacking in humour.

Instinct told her that it wasn't just the grim situation that was making Ryan look like that. He was the one who always made an effort to defuse just such an atmosphere. He seemed like a different person. Gone completely was that sparkle. The laid-back, golden-boy aura that had always seemed to cling enough to be easily resurrected.

It didn't look like Ryan intended smiling for a long time to come and Hannah didn't like it. He was being professional and she knew he would have the skills to match anything he had to face, but something was wrong. Something big was missing. The real Ryan seemed shut off. Distant.

Was it sheer arrogance to wonder if his anger at her had something to do with his demeanour?

Hannah shivered and wasn't even surprised to hear Charles's voice from close by.

'Go and get out of those overalls. Get some dry scrubs on and get a hot drink. I don't want to see you back in here for at least ten minutes.'

It did feel better, being in dry clothes. And the hot chocolate and a sandwich she found in the staffroom were wonderful.

'At least you're getting a bit of the wedding breakfast.'

Hannah smiled back at the plump woman. Susie would be surprised to see that Dora had taken off her hat. 'It's delicious,' she said. 'Thank you so much.'

'You're all doing such a wonderful job. Those poor people out there. There are a lot that are badly hurt, aren't there?'

Hannah nodded, her mouth full of the first food she had eaten since a hurried lunch too many hours ago. She had taken a moment to check on Janey's progress, to find she'd gone for a CT scan and that Alistair was planning to take her to Theatre immediately afterwards, if necessary, to relieve any pressure building from a bleed inside her skull. Emily had gone to get ready to administer an anaesthetic.

Ryan was still busy stabilising his patient, ready for the surgery Luke would have to perform to deal with the major fractures sustained.

More cases were coming in, prearranged to arrive at a steady but not overwhelming rate. Susie had hopped past on her crutches, a sheaf of papers scrunched in one hand.

'I've got to locate a new supply of O-negative blood,' she told Hannah. 'And there's so many other things to do. We're still trying to discharge people to one of the rest homes and find accommodation for everyone from the bus. You OK?'

She was, surprisingly, more than OK, thanks to the food and hot drink.

In the corner of the staffroom sat two tired-looking children. Lily was still in her flower girl's dress and CJ hadn't changed out of his small suit.

'Can we go now?' CJ asked Dora.

'We're supposed to stay here,' she replied. 'You know what they said about my house. It's not fit to be in when the cyclone comes.'

'Is it definitely coming, then?' Hannah's appetite faded and she swallowed with difficulty.

'They reckon it's going to hit us by morning. Susie's arranged some beds for the children to stay in here overnight. Dr Wetherby and CJ's parents are going to be busy all night by the look of things.'

'But you said—' CJ's lip wobbled ominously '—you *said* we could go and see if the puppies have arrived before we have to go to bed.'

'My dog's due to whelp again,' Dora explained to Hannah. 'Goodness knows why Grubby keeps letting her get in pup. It's me who ends up doing all the work.'

'Ple-ease?' begged CJ.

Dora looked at the clock. 'I guess we've got a fair few hours before the weather gets dangerous. If we went home quick and then came back again, I guess Dr Wetherby won't notice we've gone.'

'Don't tell,' CJ ordered Hannah. 'Will you?'

'I'm sure nobody will ask me,' Hannah responded. She watched as Dora took a small hand in each of hers and led the children away. A very capable woman, Dora. Hannah was sure no harm would come to the children.

And that reminded her of the shoe.

Over the next hour, as Hannah assisted in the

treatment of several people, she had two things on her mind. One of them was watching for glimpses of Ryan, to see whether he was still looking so distant and miserable.

He was. More than once he passed Hannah with barely more than a glance. Never a smile. Or a comment that might have lifted her spirits. To imagine him telling a joke seemed ridiculous. He had changed into scrubs as well so he looked like the Ryan she had always known.

She just wished she could see a flash of him behaving the way he always had.

The other thing on her mind was the shoe. At every opportunity she asked different members of the staff whether they had come across a small child amongst the patients. Someone advised her to check with one of the clerks and, sure enough, when she did, she struck gold.

'There *was* a kid. A little blonde girl,' she was told. 'Chloe, I think her name was. She had a broken arm.'

'How old was she?'

'I can't remember. Four or five.'

The right sort of age to fit a shoe the size of the one Hannah had found.

'Where would she be now?'

'I have no idea, sorry. Maybe the plaster room? It was ages ago, though. She might have been sent home.'

Except that she had no home to go to, did she?

The thoughtful frown on Hannah's face must have looked like fatigue to Charles. He rolled towards her.

'You've been on duty for more than four hours,' he said. 'It's time you took a break. At least two hours' standdown before I see you back in here, please. It's going to be a long night and it might be just the beginning of what we need you for with the way Willie's decided to behave.'

Hannah nodded. A break was exactly what she needed right now, wasn't it?

The soaked pair of overalls lay where she had left them, in the corner of the women's locker room. Nobody had had time to tidy yet. Hannah fished the shoe out of the pocket and went looking for the child she now knew existed.

Jill Shaw, the nursing director, passed her in the corridor, with her arms full of a fresh supply of IV fluids.

'Have you seen a little girl?' Hannah asked. 'About five? With blonde hair?'

'You mean Lily? I think Mrs Grubb's looking after her. She should be in the hospital somewhere.'

'No, not Lily. A child from the bus crash. I need to know if this is her shoe.' Hannah showed Jill the worn sneaker with the faded fish picture on the toe.

Jill shook her head. 'Sorry.'

Ryan emerged from the door to the toilet just behind where Jill and Hannah stood.

He still looked grim. Distant. Lines of weariness were etched deeply into his face. He looked so…serious.

Too serious for Ryan Fisher under any circumstances. It just didn't fit. Hannah could feel her heart squeeze into a painful ball. She wanted to touch him. To say something that could raise just a hint of smile or bring back just a touch of life into those dark eyes.

But she couldn't. Partly because Jill was there and mostly because Ryan wasn't even looking at her. He was looking at the object in her hand.

'For God's sake, Hannah. There are more important things to be worrying about right now than a bloody *shoe!*'

Jill raised an eyebrow as she watched him stride away. 'It's time he had a break, I think.' She turned back to Hannah. 'They're collecting all the unclaimed property in Reception. Why don't you leave it there?'

Reception was crowded. People with minor injuries from the bus crash that had been treated were waiting for transport to the emergency shelters. Other accidents attributable to the awful weather conditions were coming in in a steady stream. And there were still the people that would normally present to Emergency with the kind of injuries and illnesses they could have taken to their GP in working hours. Many of these people had been bumped well down any waiting list. Some were giving up and going home. Others were still waiting—bored, miserable and increasingly impatient.

'I don't give a stuff about bloody tourists off a bus,' an irate man was shouting at the receptionist. 'I pay my bloody taxes and I want to be seen by a doctor. *Now!* I've been waiting hours. Is this a *hospital* or what?'

Hannah gave the receptionist a sympathetic

smile. Near her desk was a sad-looking pile of wet luggage, some backpacks and other personal items like handbags, hats and sunglasses.

The angry man stormed back to his seat. Then he jumped to his feet. 'I've had enough of this,' he shouted. 'I'm bloody going home.'

Casting a glance around the waiting room, Hannah could tell nobody was sorry to see him go. She doubted there had been much wrong with him in the first place. He should see the kind of injuries that were having to wait for attention inside the department.

Hannah didn't really need a two-hour break. Maybe she should go back and help. She could leave the shoe on the pile because it probably did belong to the little girl and she might come looking for it.

Something made her turn back before she reached the pile, however. Something niggling at the back of her mind since her gaze had skimmed the more patient people still waiting for attention.

And there she was. A drowsy little blonde-headed girl, almost hidden with her mother's arms around her. She had a pink cast on her arm.

Hannah walked over to them, absurdly hopeful.

'Is this Chloe?'

The mother nodded, a worried frown creasing her forehead. 'Is there a problem? I thought we were all finished. We were just waiting for a ride to the shelter.'

'No problem,' Hannah assured her. 'I just wondered if this could be Chloe's shoe?' She held the small sneaker out but the hope that she might have solved this small mystery bothering her was fading rapidly.

Chloe was wearing some white Roman sandals. Two of them.

The little girl opened her eyes. 'That's not my shoe,' she said. 'It's the boy with the funny name's shoe.'

Hannah caught her breath. 'What boy?'

'The boy on the bus.'

'I didn't see a boy,' her mother said.

'That's because he was hiding in the back of the bus. With his friend.'

'A friend?' Hannah blinked. Surely the searchers couldn't have missed *two* children? And where were the parents? They would be frantic.

Everybody would know by now if they had missing children.

'He had a dog called Scruffy,' Chloe added. 'They were hiding so the driver wouldn't see Scruffy.'

So the friend was a dog? There had been no reports of a dog at the accident site that Hannah was aware of and that would be something people would talk about, surely? Chloe's story was beginning to seem unlikely.

'Chloe has a very good imagination,' her mother said fondly. 'Don't you, darling?' Her smile at Hannah was apologetic. 'It was a pretty long, boring bus ride.'

'I can imagine.'

'I *did* see them,' Chloe insisted. 'I went down the back of the bus when you were asleep, Mummy. His name was F-F-*Felixx*,' she said triumphantly. 'Like the cat.'

'I don't think so, darling. I've never heard of a little boy being called Felixx.'

'But it's *true,* Mummy.' Chloe was indignant. She wriggled away from the supporting arm and twisted her head sharply up to glare at her mother.

And then the small girl's eyes widened in surprise.

A split second later she went completely limp, slumped against her mother.

For a stunned moment, Hannah couldn't move. This was unreal. Talking one moment and apparently unconscious the next? Automatically she reached out to feel for a pulse in Chloe's neck.

Chloe's mother was frozen. 'What's happening?' she whispered hoarsely.

Hannah's fingers pressed deeper on the tiny neck.

Moved and pressed again.

'I don't know,' Hannah said, 'but for some reason it seems that Chloe's heart might have stopped.'

Another split second of indecision. Start CPR here in the waiting room and yell for help or get Chloe to the kind of lifesaving equipment, like a defibrillator, that she might desperately need? There was no question of what could give a better outcome.

She scooped the child into her arms. 'Come with me,' she told Chloe's mother as she ran towards the working end of the department.

'I need help,' she called as soon as she was through the door. *'Stat!'*

Ryan looked up from where he was squatting, talking to a man in a chair who had a blood-stained bandage on his hand. He took one look at Hannah's face and with a fluid movement he rose swiftly and came towards her.

'What's happened?'

'I have no idea. She just collapsed. I can't find a pulse.'

'Resus 2 is clear at the moment.' Charles was rolling beside them. 'I'll find help.'

Hannah laid Chloe on the bed. It had been well under a minute since the child had collapsed but, horribly, her instincts were screaming that they were too late. There had been something about the feel of the child in her arms.

Something completely empty.

Her fingers trembled as they reached for the ECG electrodes and stuck them in place on a tiny, frail-looking chest.

Ryan was reassessing her for a pulse and res-pirations. 'Nothing,' he said tersely. He reached for a bag-mask unit. 'What the hell is going on here?'

'Could it be a drug reaction? Anaphylaxis? What analgesia has she had for her arm?'

'Do you know if there were any prior symptoms?' Ryan had the mask over Chloe's face and was delivering enough air to make the small chest rise and then fall.

The normal-looking movement of breathing gave Hannah a ray of hope. Maybe they *weren't* too late. But then she looked up at the monitor screen to see a flat ECG trace. Not even a fibrillation they could have shocked back into a normal rhythm. She moved, automatically, to start chest compressions.

'She was fine,' she told Ryan. 'A bit drowsy but fine. She was talking to me. Telling me about the shoe and a boy who was on the bus.'

Any worries about a potentially missing child were simply not part of the picture right now.

More staff were crowding into the resus area to assist. One of the doctors, Cal, was inserting an IV line. One nurse was rolling the drugs trolley closer, the airway kit open on top of the trolley.

Charles was there. A solid presence. Beside him, Chloe's mother was standing, white faced, a nurse close by to look after her.

'An undiagnosed head injury?' Charles wondered aloud. 'A lucid period before total collapse?' He shook his head. 'Couldn't have been that dramatic.'

Ryan looked over to Chloe's mother. 'Does she have any medical conditions that you know of? Heart problems?'

'No-o-o.' The word was torn from the woman in the form of a sob. The nurse put her arms around the distraught mother. As awful as this was, it was better for a parent to see that everything possible was being done, in case they had to deal with the worst possible outcome.

Hannah kept up the chest compressions. It wasn't physically hard on someone this small. One handed. Rapid. It didn't take much pressure at all.

'Stop for a second, Hannah.'

They all looked at the screen. The disruption to the trace that the movement of CPR was causing settled.

To a flat line.

'I'm going to intubate,' Ryan decided. 'Someone hold her head for me, please?'

'I'll take over compressions.' Cal stepped up to the bed and Hannah nodded. She moved to take hold of Chloe's head and keep it in the position Ryan required.

'Oh, my God,' she murmured a moment later.

'What?' Ryan snapped. His gaze caught hers as though challenging her to say something he didn't want to hear. She had never seen anyone that determined. Ever.

'It's her neck,' Hannah said quietly. 'The way it moved. It's…' She was feeling the top of Chole's spine now, her fingers pressing carefully. Moving and pressing again. 'There's something very wrong.'

It was hardly a professional evaluation but she couldn't bring herself to say what she thought.

It fitted. Chloe must have had a fracture that had been undisplaced. She might have had a sore neck but that could have been masked by the pain relief administered for her fractured arm.

A time bomb waiting to go off. That sharp, twisting movement when she'd looked up at her mother could have displaced the broken bones. Allowed a sharp edge to sever the spinal cord.

Death would have been instantaneous.

And there was absolutely nothing any of them could do about it.

In the end, she didn't have to say anything. Her face must have said it all. Cal's hand slowed and then stopped. He stepped back from the bed.

Chloe's mother let out an agonised cry and rushed from the room. The nurse followed swiftly.

Everybody else stood silent.

Shocked.

Except for Ryan. He moved to where Cal had been standing and started chest compressions again.

And Charles rolled silently to the head of the bed where he could reach out and feel Chloe's neck for himself.

'We don't *know* her neck's broken,' Ryan said between gritted teeth. 'Not without an X-ray or CT scan. We can't just give up on her. Cal, take over again. Hannah, I want an ET tube. Five millimetre. Uncuffed.'

Nobody moved. Only Ryan, his face a frozen mask, his movements quietly desperate.

Charles dropped his hand from Chloe's neck. 'Ryan?'

The word wasn't spoken loudly but it carried the weight of an authority it would be impossible to ignore. So did the next word. *'Stop!'*

For a few seconds it looked as though Ryan might ignore the command. Keep fighting to save a life when there was absolutely no chance of success. Hannah could feel his pain. She reached out to touch his shoulder.

Ryan jerked away as though he'd been burnt. Without a glance at anyone, he turned and strode away. Long, angry strides that didn't slow as he flicked the curtain aside.

'Everybody take a break,' Charles ordered. 'Jill and I will deal with what needs to be done here.'

The shock was dreadful. Hannah could understand why Ryan hadn't been prepared to give up. If there was anything that could have been done, she would have done it herself.

Anything.

They all faced terrible things like this, working in any emergency department. That it was part of the job didn't make it easy. Somehow they had to find a way to cope or they couldn't be doing this as a career.

What was making it worse than normal for Hannah was the feeling that Ryan *couldn't* cope with this particular case. There had been something in his body language as he virtually fled from the room that spoke of real desperation. Of reaching the end of a personal, if not professional, tether.

There was no way Hannah could leave him to deal with that on his own.

She had to try and help. Or at least *be* with him. To show him that she cared. That she understood.

An ironic smile vied with the tears she was holding back.

To wallow with him, even?

CHAPTER TEN

HE WAS disappearing through the doors to the ambulance bay.

Going outside into the storm.

As scary as that was, Hannah didn't hesitate to go after him. An ambulance was unloading another patient by the time she got there and Hannah had to wait a moment as the stretcher was wheeled through the doors. Mario had done the round trip again. He was holding a bag of IV fluid aloft with one hand, steering the stretcher with the other.

'How's it going, Hannah? OK?'

Hannah could only give him a tight smile and a brief nod, unable to think of anything but her personal and urgent mission. She skirted the end of the stretcher to dash outside before the automatic doors slid shut again.

The wind caught the baggy scrub suit she was

wearing and made it billow. It teased her hair out of the band holding it back and whipped strands across her face. Her eyes stung and watered but Hannah barely registered any discomfort. It was too dark out here. The powerful hospital generators were being used for the vital power needed inside. Energy was not being wasted on outside lighting.

Where was Ryan?

Where would *she* go if she was in some kind of personal crisis and couldn't cope?

Just anywhere? Was Ryan even aware of the wild storm raging around him? Would he be thinking of his personal safety? Not likely. What if he went towards the beach? That surf had been wild and couldn't you get things like storm surges with an approaching cyclone? Like tidal waves?

If he had gone somewhere that dangerous, Hannah would still follow him. She *had* to. The bond she felt was simply too strong. If ever there was a case for following her heart, this was it.

Ryan *was* her heart.

Maybe he was heading for a safer personal space, Hannah thought as her gaze raked the swirl of leaves in the darkness and picked out the looming shapes of vehicles in the car park. He only had one space that could qualify in Crocodile Creek. His room in the doctors' house.

The room she had spent the most magical night of her life in.

Headlights from another incoming rescue vehicle sent a beam of light across the path Hannah was taking. Strong enough to show she was heading in the right direction to take her to either the beach or the house. The faded sign designating the area as the AGNES WETHERBY MEMORIAL GARDEN was tilted. Had it always been like that or was it giving up the struggle to stay upright under the duress of this storm?

Hannah wasn't about to give up.

She had to pause in the centre of the garden, just beside the sundial. She needed to catch her breath and gather her courage. The crack of a tree branch breaking free somewhere close was frightening. She would wait a few seconds in case the branch was about to fall on the path she intended to take.

It must have been instinct that alerted her to Ryan's presence in the garden. Why else would she have taken a second and much longer look at the dark shape in the corner which anyone could have taken as part of the thick hibiscus hedge behind it? Or was it because that shadow was immobile whilst the hedge was in constant motion, fuelled by relentless wind gusts?

He was sitting on a bench seat, his hands on his knees, staring blankly into the dark space in front of him.

Hannah licked lips that were dry from more than the wind.

'Ryan?'

'Go away, Hannah. Leave me alone.'

'No. I can't *do* that.' With her heart hammering, Hannah sat down beside him. Close enough to touch but she knew not to. Not yet. Ryan was too fragile. Precious. A single touch might shatter him.

So she just sat.

Very still.

They were two frozen shapes as the storm surged and howled above them.

A minute went past.

And then another.

Hannah wanted to cry. She had no idea how to help. What would Ryan do if the situation were reversed? When had she ever been this upset over a bad case at work? The closest she could think of was that little boy, Brendon, with the head injury and the dead mother and the abusive father who hadn't given a damn.

And what had Ryan done?

Told a joke. A stupid blonde joke. His way of coping or helping others to cope. Trying to make them laugh and thereby defusing an atmosphere that could be destructive.

No atmosphere could be worse than this. The pain of loving someone and being totally unable to connect. To offer comfort.

Hannah chewed the inside of her cheek as she desperately searched her memory. Had she even *heard* a blonde joke that Ryan wouldn't already know?

Maybe.

'Hey…' Surprisingly, she didn't have to shout to be heard. The wind seemed to have dropped fractionally and the hedge was were offering a small amount of protection. 'Have…have you heard the one about the blonde who went to pick up her car from the mechanic who'd been fixing it?'

There was no response from Ryan. Not a

flicker. But he'd never been put off by Hannah's deliberate indifference, had he? It took courage to continue, all the same. More courage than heading out into a potentially dangerous storm.

'She asked, "Was there much wrong with it?" and the mechanic said, "Nah, just crap in the carburettor."' Hannah had to swallow. This was so hard. How could anything be funny at a time like this? The punchline might fall like a lead balloon and she would seem shallow. Flippant. Uncaring. The things she had once accused Ryan of being. The *last* things she wanted to be seen as right now.

'And…and the blonde thought about that for a minute and then she nodded and she said, "OK…how often do I have to do that?"'

For a heartbeat, and then another, Hannah thought her fears were proving correct. The stone statue that was Ryan was still silent. Unmoving.

But then a sound escaped. A strangled kind of laughter. To Hannah's horror, however, it morphed into something else.

Ryan was *crying*.

Ghastly, racking sobs as though he had no idea *how* to cry but the sounds were being ripped from his soul.

Hannah felt tears sliding down her own face and there was no way she could prevent herself touching him now. She wrapped both her arms around him as tightly as she could, her face pressed against the back of his shoulder.

Holding him.

Trying to absorb some of the terrible grief that he seemed to be letting go.

Maybe it was Chloe's case that had caused it or maybe she'd been the straw to break the camel's back. The reason didn't matter. Ryan was hurting and if Hannah hadn't known before just how deep her love for this man went, there was no escaping that knowledge now.

She would never know how long they stayed like that. Time had no relevance. At some point, however, Ryan moved. He took Hannah's arm and pushed her away.

He couldn't bear it if Hannah felt *sorry* for him.

Adding weakness to the list of faults she already considered him to have.

He had to push her away. However comforting her touch had been, he didn't want her pity.

Searching her face in the darkness didn't reveal

what he'd been afraid to find. The shine of tears on Hannah's face was unexpected.

'Why are *you* crying?'

'Because…' Hannah gulped. 'Because *you're* crying.'

Why would she do that? There was only one reason that occurred to Ryan. She cared about him. Cared enough to be moved by his grief, even if she didn't know where it was coming from.

A very new sensation was born for Ryan right then. Wonderment. He had revealed the rawest of emotions. Exposed a part of himself he'd never shared with another living soul and Hannah had not only witnessed it, she had accepted it.

Was *sharing* it even.

Oh, man! This was huge. As big as the storm currently raging over their heads.

Bigger even.

Ryan sniffed and scrubbed his nose with the palm of his hand. He made an embarrassed kind of sound.

'First time for everything, I guess.'

'You mean this is the *first* time you've ever cried?'

'Yeah.' Ryan sniffed again and almost managed a smile. The grief had drained away and left a curious sort of peace. Had the crying done that? Or Hannah's touch? A combination of both maybe. 'Well, since I was about five or six anyway.'

'Oh…' And Hannah was smiling back at him. A gentle smile that was totally without any kind of judgement. 'I'm glad I was here.'

'Yeah…' It was still difficult to swallow but the lump in his throat seemed different. A happy lump rather than an agonised one. How could that be? 'Me, too.'

They listened to the wind for a moment. Felt the fat drops of rain ping against their bare arms.

'I'm sorry, Ryan,' Hannah said.

'What for?'

'Lots of things.'

'Like what?'

'Like that we couldn't save Chloe.'

'We could have, if we'd only known.' Ryan felt the weight of sadness pulling him down again but he knew he wouldn't go as far as he had. Never again. Hannah had stopped his fall. Made something right in the world again. 'It shouldn't have happened.'

'No, of course it shouldn't, but I can see why it did. If there hadn't been so many injuries it would have been standard protocol to check her out a lot more carefully. To collar and backboard her until X-rays were done, given the mechanism of injury. But she was part of the walking wounded group. She only complained about her sore arm.'

'Tunnel vision.'

'Not entirely. With so many to care for, you don't have time to think outside the square. Tick the boxes that don't seem urgent. Anyway, it happened and it's dreadful and I know how you must feel.' A tentative smile curved Hannah's lips. 'I'm available for a spot of wallowing.'

Ryan shook his head. 'I don't do wallowing, you know that.' He snorted softly. 'Hell, if I went down that track with the kind of material I've got to keep me going, I'd end up like a character in some gloomy Russian novel. Chloe *did* get to me more than usual, though. Too close to home.'

'I don't understand.'

Of course she didn't. Why had Ryan thought that keeping his private life private would make things easier?

'I've got a niece,' he told her. 'Michaela. She's six and blonde and it could have been her in there instead of Chloe. Not that there's anything that could save Mikki so to have another little girl that didn't *have* to die and still did seemed just too unfair to be acceptable.'

'Mikki *has* to die?'

'It's inevitable. She's got neuroaxonal dystrophy. It's an autosomal recessive genetic disease and it's incredibly cruel. They seem perfectly normal at birth and even for the first year or two, and then there's a steady deterioration until they die a few years later. Mikki can't move any more. She can't see or talk. She can still hear and she can smile. She's got the most gorgeous smile.'

When had Hannah's hand slipped into his like that? Ryan returned the squeeze.

'I love that kid,' he said quietly. 'She's got a couple of older brothers but she was special right from day one.'

'And she lives here, in Australia?'

'Brisbane. She's my older brother's child. He's taking it hard and it's putting a big strain on the marriage. He's a bit like me, I guess—not good at sharing the hard stuff in life. Easier to bottle it up and have a laugh about something meaningless.'

'Like a joke.' Hannah was nodding.

'Yeah. Shallow, isn't it?'

'You're not shallow, Ryan. You care more than anyone I've ever met. You've just been good at hiding it.' She cleared her throat. 'So Mikki's the reason you come back to Australia so often?'

'Yeah. I try to be there whenever things get really tough or when she has a hospital appointment. I can explain things again to her parents later.'

'It's a huge commitment.'

'I would have moved there to make it easier to be supportive but my parents live in Auckland. Dad had a stroke a couple of years ago. Quite a bad one and Mum's finding it harder to cope. So there I was in Sydney, commuting one way and then another. The travel time was playing havoc with my career so I had to choose one city and the job in Auckland happened to come up first. It doesn't seem to take any longer to get to Brisbane from Auckland than it did from Sydney and I'm only doing half the travelling I used to do.'

Hannah's smile was rueful. 'And I was thinking that Michaela was a girlfriend. Or an ex-wife.'

Ryan snorted. 'For one thing, any wife of mine would never become an "ex". For another, I haven't had time in my life for a relationship for years. Who would, with the kind of family commitments I've got?'

'But you go out with everyone. You never miss a party.'

'I'm in a new city. I need to find friends. Sometimes I just need to escape and do normal, social things. I still feel lonely but if you can't find some fun somewhere in life, it takes all the sense out of struggling along with the bad bits.'

'I can't believe I accused you of being shallow, Ryan. I'm really, really sorry.'

'Don't be. I can see why you did. I've never told anyone at work what goes on in my private life. I had a feeling that if I started I'd never be able to stop and it would be too hard. I'd end up a mess and people would just feel sorry for me. I've got too much pride to take that on board.'

'*I* don't feel sorry for you.'

'You don't?'

'No.'

'What *do* you feel, Han?'

'I…feel a lot.' Hannah was looking down, avoiding his gaze. 'I'm…in love with you, Ryan.'

There.

She'd said it.

Opened her heart right up.

Made herself as vulnerable as it was possible to get, but what choice had she had? There was no escaping the truth and she couldn't live a lie.

And hadn't Ryan made himself just as vulnerable? He hadn't cried in front of anyone in his adult life. He could have hidden it from her. Stormed off and shut her out before he let himself go. He'd been exercising control over his emotions for year after year. He could have done the same for a minute or two longer.

But he hadn't. At some level he had trusted her enough to show her who he really was.

An utterly amazing, caring, committed man.

How could she have been so wrong about him?

Ryan deserved nothing less than the absolute truth from her, no matter how painful the repercussions.

She was too afraid to look at him. It was too

dark to be able to interpret expressions accurately enough in any case.

She didn't need to be able to see, though. She could feel the touch under her chin as Ryan tilted her face up to meet his.

Could feel the touch of his lips on her own, the rain-slicked smoothness of her skin against the grating stubble of a jaw that hadn't been near a razor since what was now yesterday.

The kiss was as gentle as it was powerful.

It told Hannah she didn't need to be afraid. Ryan understood that vulnerability and he wasn't going to break her trust if he could help it.

The first words he spoke when he drew away had to be the most important Hannah would ever hear.

She wasn't disappointed.

'I love you, too, Hannah Jackson.'

The rain was pelting down now. Ryan smoothed damp strands of hair back from Hannah's forehead.

'We need to find somewhere dry,' he said.

Hannah laughed. Incredible as it seemed, in the wake of what they had just been through and with the prospect of more gruelling hours of work ahead, there was joy to be found in life. In each other.

'Where have I heard that before?'

'We're on a break. We've got two hours to escape. To forget about the world and be dry. And warm. And safe.' Ryan kissed her again. 'You'll always be safe with me, Hannah. I promise you that.'

She took his face between both her hands. 'And so will you be,' she vowed. 'With me.'

She let Ryan pull her to her feet and she smiled. 'I'd like to go somewhere dry with you. Very much.' Her smile broadened. 'Even though I already know how good our rapport is.'

'Yeah…' Ryan growled. 'I'm *fun.*'

'I didn't mean that, you know. It was so much more than that. I was just trying to protect myself.'

'From *me?*' Ryan sounded baffled.

'Yes. I thought it was far too dangerous to fall for someone like you.'

'Who, exactly, is someone like me?'

'Oh, you know. Someone fun. Clever. Exciting. Great looking. Too good to be true.'

'I'm someone like that?' Now he sounded very pleasantly surprised.

'Someone exactly like that. A bit too much like the man my mother fell head over heels in love with. And the one that Susie fell in love with. And they both got bored or hadn't been genuine in the first place, and it was me who had to pick up all the pieces. Do you know how many pieces you can get out of *two* broken hearts?'

'No. How many?'

'Heaps,' Hannah said firmly. 'Way *too* many.'

Ryan pulled her to a stop. Pulled her into his arms. 'Your heart's going to stay in one piece if I have anything to do with it,' he said seriously. 'I'm going to make it my mission in life.'

The promise was too big. Hannah didn't want anything to make her cry again. She had to smile and try to lighten the emotional overload. 'Could be a full-time job.'

'I intend to make sure it is.'

'It might be a lifetime career.'

'I certainly hope so.'

'Of course, there's always the prospect of promotion.'

'Really? What kind of promotion?'

Why had she started this? Suddenly it didn't

seem like a joke. 'Oh, maybe being an emergency department consultant?'

'I might not get that job. I've heard that I've got some pretty stiff competition.'

Hannah's heart was doing some curious flip-flops. 'I might not mind very much if I don't get that job.'

'Why not?'

'I might have more important things in my life than my career.'

Ryan was smiling. 'Such as?' He raised a hopeful eyebrow. 'You mean *me?*'

Hannah nodded shyly. 'Maybe even... How would you feel about a promotion to being a father?'

'Dr Jackson! Is that a proposal?'

'I don't know.' Hannah caught her bottom lip between her teeth. 'Would you like it to be?'

'No.'

Hannah's heart plummeted. But then she saw the gleam of Ryan's teeth.

'I'm old-fashioned,' he announced. 'If there's to be any proposing going on around here, *I'll* do it.'

And that's exactly what he did. In the heart of

a tropical storm, in the middle of a garden, just beside a sundial, Ryan got down on one knee, holding both of Hannah's hands in his own.

'I love you.' He had to shout because the wind had risen again to snatch his words away and the rain was thundering down and the wail of a siren close by rose and fell.

'I love you, Hannah. You are the only person in existence that I can really be myself with. The only time in my life I felt no hint of being alone was when I had you in my bed. You make me whole. I don't ever want to live without having you by my side. Will you—please—marry me?'

'Oh, I think so.' Hannah sank to her knees on the wet flagstones of the path. 'I love you, too, Ryan.' It was easier to hear now that their heads were close together again. 'You are the only person in existence that I've ever…had such a good rapport with.' They were grinning at each other now, at the absurdity of choosing this particular place and time to make such declarations. Then Hannah's smile faded. It had just happened this way and because it had, it was perfect. 'Yes,' she said slowly. 'I would love to marry you.'

Ryan shook the raindrops from his hair after giving Hannah a lingering, wonderful kiss.

'Can we go somewhere dry now?'

Hannah nodded but the wail of the siren was still going and she hesitated when Ryan helped her up and then tugged on her hand.

'What's up, babe?'

'I can't stop thinking about it.'

'The bus crash? The cyclone that's on its way that we'd better find some shelter from pretty damn quick?'

'No…the shoe.'

'Did Chloe really tell you there was a boy on the bus?'

'Yes.'

'And you believe her?'

'Yes.'

'We'd better find Harry or someone, then, and let them know.'

Hannah nodded. 'I'd feel a lot better if we did. Do you mind?'

'Why should I mind?'

'It'll take a bit longer to find somewhere dry. To have that break.'

'Babe, we've got all the time in the world to

work on our rapport.' Ryan had his arm around Hannah, sheltering her from some of the wind and rain. They had to bend forward to move against the force of the elements and get themselves back towards Crocodile Creek Base Hospital's emergency department.

But it felt so different than when Hannah had been going in the opposite direction on her search for Ryan. With his strength added to her own, she knew there was nothing she wouldn't be prepared to face.

Ryan paused once more as they reached the relative shelter of the ambulance bay. 'It *is* real, isn't it?'

'What, the cyclone? Sure feels like it.'

'No, I mean, how we feel about each other. The love.'

'As real as this storm,' Hannah assured him. 'And just as powerful.'

'What happens when the sun comes out?'

'We'll be in a dry place.' Hannah smiled. 'Having fun.'

Ryan looked over her shoulder through the doors into the emergency department. 'I don't think fun's on the agenda for a while yet.'

'No.' Hannah followed the direction of his gaze. Chloe was still somewhere in there. So were a lot of other people who needed attention. And when the aftermath of the bus crash had been mopped up, they could be on standby for the first casualties from a cyclone.

'It's not going to be easy.'

'No.'

'Are you up for it?'

'With you here as well? Of course I am. We can do this, Ryan. We'll be doing it together.'

'Together is good. Oh, and, Han?'

'Yes?'

'Can I have that blonde joke? The one about the carburettor? It was great.'

'You can have anything and everything I have to give,' Hannah told him. 'Always.'

Ryan took hold of her hand once more and they both turned towards the automatic doors. Ready to step back into a place that needed them both almost as much as they needed each other.

'Same,' Ryan said softly. 'For ever.'

MEDICAL™

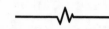

Large Print

Titles for the next six months...

April

THE ITALIAN COUNT'S BABY	Amy Andrews
THE NURSE HE'S BEEN WAITING FOR	Meredith Webber
HIS LONG-AWAITED BRIDE	Jessica Matthews
A WOMAN TO BELONG TO	Fiona Lowe
WEDDING AT PELICAN BEACH	Emily Forbes
DR CAMPBELL'S SECRET SON	Anne Fraser

May

THE MAGIC OF CHRISTMAS	Sarah Morgan
THEIR LOST-AND-FOUND FAMILY	Marion Lennox
CHRISTMAS BRIDE-TO-BE	Alison Roberts
HIS CHRISTMAS PROPOSAL	Lucy Clark
BABY: FOUND AT CHRISTMAS	Laura Iding
THE DOCTOR'S PREGNANCY BOMBSHELL	Janice Lynn

June

CHRISTMAS EVE BABY	Caroline Anderson
LONG-LOST SON: BRAND-NEW FAMILY	Lilian Darcy
THEIR LITTLE CHRISTMAS MIRACLE	Jennifer Taylor
TWINS FOR A CHRISTMAS BRIDE	Josie Metcalfe
THE DOCTOR'S VERY SPECIAL CHRISTMAS	Kate Hardy
A PREGNANT NURSE'S CHRISTMAS WISH	Meredith Webber

MILLS & BOON®
Pure reading pleasure

0308 LP 2P P1 Medic

MEDICAL™

Large Print

July

THE ITALIAN'S NEW-YEAR MARRIAGE WISH — Sarah Morgan

THE DOCTOR'S LONGED-FOR FAMILY — Joanna Neil

THEIR SPECIAL-CARE BABY — Fiona McArthur

THEIR MIRACLE CHILD — Gill Sanderson

SINGLE DAD, NURSE BRIDE — Lynne Marshall

A FAMILY FOR THE CHILDREN'S DOCTOR — Dianne Drake

August

THE DOCTOR'S BRIDE BY SUNRISE — Josie Metcalfe

FOUND: A FATHER FOR HER CHILD — Amy Andrews

A SINGLE DAD AT HEATHERMERE — Abigail Gordon

HER VERY SPECIAL BABY — Lucy Clark

THE HEART SURGEON'S SECRET SON — Janice Lynn

THE SHEIKH SURGEON'S PROPOSAL — Olivia Gates

September

THE SURGEON'S FATHERHOOD SURPRISE — Jennifer Taylor

THE ITALIAN SURGEON CLAIMS HIS BRIDE — Alison Roberts

DESERT DOCTOR, SECRET SHEIKH — Meredith Webber

A WEDDING IN WARRAGURRA — Fiona Lowe

THE FIREFIGHTER AND THE SINGLE MUM — Laura Iding

THE NURSE'S LITTLE MIRACLE — Molly Evans

MILLS & BOON®

Pure reading pleasure

0308 LP 2P P2 Medical